Praise f(

"Adrian has a gift for drawing her readers deeper and deeper into the amazing world she creates."

—Fresh Fiction

"With an Adrian novel, readers are assured of plenty of dangerous thrills and passionate chills."

—RT Book Reviews

"Nothing beats good writing and that is what ultimately makes Lara Adrian stand out amongst her peers . . . Adrian doesn't hold back with the intensity or the passion."

—Under the Covers

"Adrian has a style of writing that creates these worlds that are so realistic and believable . . . the characters are so rich and layered . . . the love stories are captivating and often gut-wrenching . . . edge of your seat stuff!"

—Scandalicious Book Reviews

"Adrian compels readers to get hooked on her storylines."
—Romance Reviews Today

Praise for Lara Adrian's books

"Adrian's strikingly original Midnight Breed series delivers an abundance of nail-biting suspenseful chills, red-hot sexy thrills, an intricately built world, and realistically complicated and conflicted protagonists, whose happily-ever-after ending proves to be all the sweeter after what they endure to get there."

—Booklist (starred review)

"(The Midnight Breed is) a well-written, action-packed series that is just getting better with age."

—Fiction Vixen

Praise for
FOR 100 DAYS

"I wish I could give this more than 5 stars! Lara Adrian not only dips her toe into this genre with flare, she will take it over . . . I have found my new addiction, this series."

—The Sub Club Books

"There are twists that I want to say that I expect from a Lara Adrian book, and I say that because with any Adrian book you read, you know there's going to be a complex storyline. Adrian simply does billionaires better."

—Under the Covers

"This book had me completely addicted from page one!! There were several twists and turns throughout this super steamy read and I was surprised by how much mystery/suspense was woven in. Loved that! If you're looking for the perfect summer read, look no further than this book!"

—Steph and Chris Book Blog

"I have been searching and searching for the next book boyfriend to leave a lasting impression. You know the ones: where you own the paperbacks, eBooks and the audible versions…This is that book. For those of you who are looking for your next Fifty Fix, look no further. I know, I know—you have heard the phrase before! Except this time, it's the truth and I will bet the penthouse on it."

—Mile High Kink Book Club

"For 100 Days is a sexy, sizzling, emotion-filled delight. It completely blew me away!"

—J. Kenner, New York Times bestselling author

Praise for
FOR 100 NIGHTS

"For 100 Nights is an erotic delight that will have you on the edge of your seat! An instant addiction and a complete escape, with an intriguing storyline and an ending that will leave you gasping for air. This series has quickly become one of my favorites!"

—Shayna Renee's Spicy Reads

"There is only one word that can adequately describe For 100 Nights: PHENOMENAL. For 100 Days was one of my favourite books of last year and this book has topped that. . . . Move over because there is a new queen of erotica on the charts and you don't want to miss her."

—The Sub Club Books

"If you're looking for a hot new contemporary romance along the lines of Sylvia Day's Crossfire series then you're not going to want to miss this series!"

—Feeling Fictional

"Lara Adrian has once again wowed me with her writing. She has created a complex erotic romance that has layers upon layers for both of her characters. Their passion for one another is romantic, sizzling, and a little bit naughty. Lara has added intrigue and suspense that keeps the reader completely involved. Each small revelation is leading to an explosive conclusion. I cannot wait for the third and final book, For 100 Reasons, to release."

—Smut Book Junkie Reviews

Other books by Lara Adrian

Midnight Breed series

Midnight Breed Spinoff

Hunter Legacy Series
Born of Darkness
Hour of Darkness
Edge of Darkness

Historical Romances

Dragon Chalice Series
Heart of the Hunter
Heart of the Flame
Heart of the Dove

Warrior Trilogy
White Lion's Lady
Black Lion's Bride
Lady of Valor

Lord of Vengeance

Paranormal Romance

Masters of Seduction Series
Merciless: House of Gravori
Priceless: House of Ebarron (novella)

FOR 100 REASONS

A 100 Series Novel

NEW YORK TIMES BESTSELLING AUTHOR

LARA ADRIAN

ISBN: 1974030636
ISBN-13: 978-1974030637

FOR 100 REASONS
© 2017 by Lara Adrian, LLC
Cover design © 2022 by Lara Adrian

www.LaraAdrian.com

Available in ebook, trade paperback, and unabridged audiobook editions.

For 100
Reasons

1

Paris

I tried to warn her that I wasn't a good man.

From the very beginning, I told her she deserved someone better. Now, she knows it's true.

Selfish, ruthless bastard. That's what I am, what I always have been. I've never made a secret of that fact. Never apologized for it, either. Hell, it's the only way I know how to survive.

When I see something I desire, I don't waste time waiting for it to land at my feet. I reach for it. I take what I want, by fair means or foul. And more than a year ago—when I caught my first glimpse of Avery Ross—what I wanted above anything else was her.

For the past five months, she's been mine.

Long enough for me to realize how incredible she is.

Long enough for her to turn me inside out. To make me forget what it was to crave any other woman but her.

Christ, what have I done?

In a few short months, this beautiful, broken, infinitely brave woman has made me want something I've never had nor ever dreamed I would need.

Now, she's gone.

I feel her absence as if a piece of me has been ripped away from my body. And the worst of it is I have no one to blame but myself.

On a snarled curse, I slam my palm on the steering wheel of my Mercedes AMG GT as the traffic ahead of me on A1 out of Paris creeps at a virtual standstill. A slim opening appears beside me on the freeway. I seize it, grimacing as I make a reckless dodge through the clogged rivers of compact cars, taxis, tourist vans, and delivery vehicles that stand between me and the Charles de Gaulle Airport.

"Go, damn it!" I lay on the horn, furious. Desperate to keep moving. I have to reach her before she's gone for good. "Out of my fucking way!"

Zig-zagging past the slower moving vehicles, I gun the 450-plus horsepower engine and roar over a brief space of open highway. A few hundred yards ahead, that gap closes up. Another goddamned standstill.

Fuck it. I veer onto the concrete shoulder, speeding along it like a man possessed.

In truth, I *am* a man possessed. I have been ever since I set my sights on Avery.

Her face haunts me as I navigate the congested traffic heading toward the exit for the airport. All I can see is her tear-filled green eyes looking up at me in shock—in despisement—over the way I'd betrayed her.

You set everything up, Nick! You took my life apart piece by piece until you had me in your hands. In your bed.

All true.

I couldn't deny anything she'd said back at my flat where we made love only a couple of hours ago. Nothing I said could make her understand. I don't know if she'll ever forgive me.

In a handful of seconds she went from loving me to hating me. As she'd shoved past me, determined to leave, I told myself I had earned every bit of her scorn, every bit of this pain.

And when she ran from my place with her purse and passport in hand, into a taxi that sped her away, I told myself the fairest thing to do—the only right thing—was to let her go.

Yeah, fuck that.

Since when have I treated her fairly? Since when have I concerned myself with doing the right thing by her?

I'll be damned if I'm going to start now. Not when she's the one person in this world who means anything to me. The only woman I've ever truly loved.

I swerve in to the airport entrance and race for the departures terminal. A French policeman shouts at me as I leap out of the car and leave it unattended at the curb.

Ignoring the sharp whistle and the barked orders to stop—first in French, then in English—I run into the busy terminal and head directly for the AirFrance ticket counter. If Avery intends to fly home to New York City, odds are she's found an available seat on one of the frequent nonstops taking off from this hub.

The first-class line is a dozen deep with customers

who scoff and grumble and curse at me as I bypass all of them to reach the counter attendant. She gives me a wary look, her gaze darting over my shoulder where the police officer continues to shout at me.

"Sir, you cannot jump the line. There are other people waiting—"

"I need to find someone," I tell her, my voice low and tight with urgency. And, yes, desperation. "Please, I need your help. It's important."

"You there!" The officer's call sounds nearer now. And he's pissed. "Monsieur, I am speaking to you."

I glance back and see that the disruption has attracted the attention of a pair of uniformed French soldiers. Maroon berets and green camouflage move in from posts at the other end of the ticketing area. The situation is escalating quickly.

I'm sure I look unsettling, even dangerous or unstable, especially given the current state of unease in the world. But I don't have time to deal with anxious security patrols or aggravated cops. I need to find Avery and keep her from getting on that plane. Hell, I'll search the whole damned airport if that's what it takes.

"Monsieur!" The shout comes from one of the soldiers approaching me from behind now.

"Ah, fuck this." I pivot in front of the counters and head for the security line.

People move out of my path like a receding wave, wary looks and whispers left in my wake. Children drawn close to their parents as I pass. I'm causing a scene, probably on my way toward an international incident, but I don't care.

I duck under a length of security tape just as a firm hand latches onto my arm. "Sir, I wouldn't do this if I were you."

The largest of the French soldiers holds me in an iron grasp. His partner steps in on my other side, while a third blocks me from the front. Their faces are stern, all three gazes unblinking and prepared to take me down.

Each second I'm delayed here is a second closer to losing Avery. When I speak, it's through gritted teeth. "Let me go. I have to get through."

"No, sir." The mammoth in front of me shakes his dark head. "You've gone far enough."

I know there's no getting past these men, nor their guns. I've already lost. I'm too late to make Avery listen, even if she somehow granted me the chance.

On a roar, I fight against the hold on my arm. I wrench loose, fueled by fury and a sawing ache in my chest that's too big to be contained.

It explodes out of me on a growl. My fist flies at the same time, connecting with the soldier's jaw in front of me. His head rocks back on his shoulders, but only for a second.

When the hammer of his answering blow smashes into my face, I savor the pain. I've earned it after all. And for the briefest moment—before my vision goes dark and the hard concrete floor comes up to greet me—I tell myself that Avery deserves this chance to fly away and escape me.

She deserves everything that I can never give her.

She deserves to be free, to live her life without me.

2

New York
One year later

Avery, if you have a moment, the magazine would like to get a few more photos for your interview."

"Okay. Thank you, Rachel." From within the small throng of art critics and collectors circled around me, I nod at the publicist who's been hired to help me navigate tonight's invitation-only reception. "Will you all excuse me, please?"

Slipping away, I follow her through the thick, buzzing crowd that fills the newly opened modern art gallery at one of the city's most prestigious private universities. The high-ceilinged, open-concept space is packed, vibrating with energy. Soft music plays from the string quartet set up near the open cocktail bar. Mingled conversations swell from all directions, punctuated here and there by the soft clink of crystal glasses.

And on the soaring white walls that surround the gathering, paintings from contemporary masters hang alongside works from promising new talents and Avant-garde outsiders, most of whom are in attendance tonight.

It's hard to believe I'm actually a guest at this elegant event, let alone that I'm here because one of my pieces has been acquired for the university's collection.

"Ms. Ross, can you tell us what you're working on now?" The question comes at me from somewhere to my right, accompanied by a hand holding a cell phone camera in my face. Rachel is there in an instant, smoothly deflecting for me.

"Ken, you'll have to wait to find out, just like everyone else." Smiling at the disappointed reporter, she steers me away from him. "How are you holding up tonight?"

"Good. I'm having a great time."

"It's okay, you can be honest with me. You hate all the attention, don't you?" She winks at me as we walk. "After the price your most recent painting commanded, you should be getting used to it. Everyone wants a piece of you now."

I try to ignore the shudder that rakes me at the thought of being the focus of so much curiosity. I spent most of my life hiding from my past and the monsters who inhabited it, so I can't imagine a time when I'll ever be comfortable standing in the spotlight.

Thankfully, none of these people here tonight can see inside me to the terrified, damaged child I once was or the many ugly secrets I had to keep in order to survive.

Only one person glimpsed deep enough to really see me, and for the past year I've been doing my damnedest to forget him. Not that it's been easy.

For the short handful of months we were together, Dominic Baine had consumed me. He had been my everything—or so I'd foolishly believed. In reality, Nick had been playing me for a fool from the moment I first met him.

No, I remind myself harshly. He had been playing me even longer than that.

From the time he saw one of my paintings hanging in his gallery, Dominion, nearly two years ago now and decided he had to have me. But the joke was on him, wasn't it?

He didn't realize I was damaged goods.

He didn't know about the secrets I had been keeping all my life. The abuse and the shame, the obfuscation.

The blood and the death.

I wish I could take some satisfaction in how I deceived him too. When I think about how I hid my past from him, how I allowed him to risk his own life to protect me when that horrid past eventually came to collect on my debts, all I taste is regret.

I wish I could take it back. I wish I could reset the clock and start over.

That was the reason Nick had taken me to Paris—to reset the clock. Or so he claimed.

With my sins all bared to him and no more secrets to stand in our way, I thought Paris would be a new beginning. And it was. I just had no idea we'd be starting over apart.

I didn't want to believe it was over, but I couldn't stay.

Not after what he did, systematically manipulating me, controlling every detail of my life as if I were nothing but a pawn being moved around on his chessboard, until he had me right where he wanted me.

Conquered.

Owned.

His.

Worst of all, Nick played me so masterfully, I fell completely, helplessly—*stupidly*—in love with him.

When it all fell apart in Paris last summer, I thought the pain would kill me. How it didn't, I have no idea.

Throwing myself into my work has helped.

Moving out of Manhattan has helped too. The 1940s townhouse I bought in the Forest Hills neighborhood of Queens two months ago could not be more different from the towering glamour of the Park Place building where I spent so much time with Nick.

It's hard to go anywhere in the city and not think of him, not be bombarded with unwanted memories of all the places we explored together. All of the dark, erotic pleasures we shared.

Ancient history.

I push thoughts of him to the back of my mind as Rachel leads me over to the waiting photographer from the art magazine and the woman who interviewed me earlier tonight. They position me in front of my painting and as the camera clicks away I do my best to look like the confident, coolly unaffected artist they all seem to expect.

"Thank you again for your time, Avery." The reporter walks over and shakes my hand after the photos are taken. "We're planning a series of artist spotlights later this year. In addition to featuring your work, we'd like to talk to you more in depth about some of your influences, your early life, things that have shaped your remarkable work. If you're interested, we'd love to add you to the program."

"Oh. Um . . ."

"Of course," Rachel interjects. "She'd be happy to participate."

The two women exchange contact information and make arrangements to talk next week about scheduling for the article.

"That really wasn't necessary," I tell Rachel once we're alone.

"Yes, it really was." She purses her lips and looks at me over the rims of her tortoise-shell glasses. "Kathryn hired me to take care of you tonight because she couldn't be here. She'd never forgive me if I let a great opportunity like that slip through your fingers."

I nod begrudgingly. Kathryn Tremont has become a dear friend this past year. She also happens to be one of the wealthiest women in New York and a force to be reckoned with in the art world. As much as I dislike accepting favors or being managed, I know Kathryn is only trying to help me because she cares.

And Rachel is only trying to do her job.

Her phone chimes with an incoming call. "Sorry, I have to take this. Don't forget, the dean will be inviting you and the other artists up on stage to say a few words before his closing remarks."

I nod, but she's already pivoted away, immersed in conversation on her phone.

I spend an awkward minute standing by myself in

front of my painting, wishing I had friends with me at the reception. Not that I'm completely alone. In addition to Rachel, my date is here somewhere, too, although I don't see Brandon's ginger curls and ruddy cheeks among the sea of attendees. I shift on my high-heeled sandals, arms crossed over the front of my black Valentino cocktail dress as I crane my neck to scan the crowded gallery.

How long has he been gone, anyway? It seems like an hour since he left to fetch drinks for us. As much as Brandon likes to chat, it wouldn't surprise me if he hasn't even made it to the bar yet. God knows I could use a dash of liquid courage before I'm due on the stage.

Since I have a few moments to myself, I figure I'll go in search of my erstwhile date or an adult beverage, whichever I locate first. Just as I step into the cluster of party guests, a wall of firm, warm muscle seems to materialize in front of me.

We collide only briefly, my palm splaying against an unbuttoned, bespoke black suit jacket and the crisp white shirt beneath it. Heat sears me on contact, as if my senses recognize the danger even before my brain can engage. I glance up into sharp cerulean blue eyes that still hold the power to strip me to the bone.

"Nick."

My voice is too quiet, rough with the shock of seeing him for the first time since Paris.

New York is immense, but to think we've gone a year in and out of the same city without running into each other must be some kind of miracle. A blessing, as far as I'm concerned. Of course, I've done my best to avoid him, staying away from the places I know he frequents, making sure the chances of our paths crossing are next to nil.

Now this.

Even though I understood there would come a time when our paths would likely cross again, the sight of him is as powerful as a physical blow. That crown of thick, raven-dark hair that gleams under the soft gallery lights overhead. That strong, straight nose and impossibly square jaw, as sharp as a blade and shadowed with the rough beginnings of his beard.

And, most devastating of all, those sinfully lush lips that have been on every inch of my body, and have whispered such dirty, wonderful things to me before I realized everything he said was based on a lie.

He stares down at me, his gaze intense but unreadable from beneath inky black brows. "Hello, Avery."

As surprised as I am to find him standing in front of me, I know my narrowed glare is ripe with suspicion, if not blatant accusation. All justified, considering how disastrously things ended between us. "What are you doing here, Nick?"

"I received an invitation, like everyone else."

That sinfully deep voice vibrates along my nerve endings, generating unwanted heat and an awareness I don't care to acknowledge. I edge backward, craving space. If I had any less pride, I'd be tempted to bolt for the nearest exit.

But I have every right to be here. It's Nick who's the interloper.

"I suppose you didn't know I'd be here too."

"Actually, I didn't. Lily made the arrangements. For some reason, she neglected to mention the guest list of attending artists. I'll be taking the matter up with her in the morning."

He doesn't sound pleased with his assistant, and I have to wonder if the impeccably efficient Lily Fontana could have lost some of her edge the past year. I doubt it, but I can't imagine why she'd think putting Nick and me within a city block of each other was anything but a bad idea.

"I apologize, Avery. If I had known you'd be here, I promise you, I wouldn't have come."

God, he really means that. It's hard to deny his earnestness. For all his past deceptions, I recognize his honesty now. I'm not sure why I don't feel more relief, some sense of satisfaction that he can at least acknowledge the wreckage that lies between us.

Instead, all I feel as we stand together for the first time in so long is the racing beat of my heart. The streaks of uninvited, unwanted awareness. The dull ache of regret over everything that might have been.

Nick's gaze takes a while to leave mine. When it does, his eyes flick past my shoulder to the painting hanging on the wall behind me. He moves toward it, studying the canvas. My breath lodges in the center of my chest as I watch him take in the large abstract depiction of silvery feathers, turbulent blue water, and flame-filled orange sky.

He swivels his head toward me, a flicker of surprise in his expression. *"Icarus."*

The painting is more than the myth, and we both know it. I acknowledge with a nod.

He hasn't seen it before, even though I first began working on this piece soon after we took our first getaway together. Our Florida Keys sail aboard Nick's beautiful boat, *Icarus*, seems like a hundred years ago now. So much has happened since then. So many lies between us, so much pain.

"I've been carrying it around with me for the past year. I figured it was finally time to let go."

Time to let *us* go. I don't have to say the words out loud. Nick's gaze holds mine, penetrating and intense, still powerful enough to cleave me wide open if I'm not careful.

But I am careful. I have to be, especially with him.

It's been a year since I spoke to him—since I've been close enough to feel the warmth of his body and breathe in the spicy, intoxicating scent of him, which even now seems to trip all of my senses. A year since I've known Nick's touch, yet I feel the memory of it as if I had been in his arms only yesterday.

I don't want the memories anymore. He can't possibly know how hard I've worked to move past them, to get on with my life after he shattered my heart with his betrayal.

But he does know.

I can see that knowledge in every nuance of his handsome face. I see a hundred questions in his eyes, a hundred things we both should have said in Paris. Things we need to say to each other now, but probably never will.

"You look good, Avery." He studies me as he speaks, and I'm not sure if it's surprise or disappointment I hear in his subdued tone. "I'm happy for all your success. The gallery showings, the accolades from the press and critics. The six-figure acquisition of your last painting. Congratulations, by the way. You're headed for even bigger things, I have no doubt. I'm impressed."

And I'm astonished. I can't deny that his praise

affects me, but I'm more taken aback to hear that he's aware of everything that's happened with my career this past year. Evidently, he's been paying attention.

I'd be lying to myself to pretend I haven't been curious about him too. Not that he's made it easy to ferret out even the smallest information since we've been apart. Nick's reputation for privacy in his personal life is almost as notable as his staggering net worth. The "shadow mogul" has been practically invisible the past year. Not a single photo in the media, not a hint of gossip in the society pages or the Internet.

In the absence of facts, I indulged in countless spiteful fantasies about him. Imagining Nick haggard and despondent, with an overgrown, unkempt beard and midsection paunch. Reveling in the idea that he might be suffering as profoundly as I had after I returned home from Paris alone, an inconsolable, shredded mess.

But Nick has never looked better. Still flawlessly fit, devastatingly gorgeous. And he's staring at me as if he can see every imperfection in me, every fissure in my carefully constructed facade. As if I'm still the heartbroken, foolish woman he treated like his plaything.

The woman he once claimed he loved.

"Are you happy, Avery?"

"Happy?" The question catches me off guard, another of his specialties. I force a smile and a nonchalant shrug. "As you pointed out yourself, things have never been better."

"That's not really an answer."

A scoff erupts out of me before I can hold it back. "The way I recall it, you're the one owing the answers, not me."

"You're right." He grunts, sounding almost contrite.

"You didn't seem ready for anything I had to say then. Are you now?"

"You're a little late, Nick. None of it matters anymore."

"Would it have then?"

"No."

It's the truth, even though I've told myself he should have at least tried. He should have come after me that day in Paris or any of the hundreds that followed. Some pathetic part of me had been certain he'd come after me. Dominic Baine isn't one to let something that belongs to him slip through his fingers.

He should have forced me to listen. Regardless of my capacity to forgive him, he should have explained why he chose me to manipulate the way he did.

But he did none of those things.

He let me go.

He watched me walk out the door of his flat and out of his life, and in all this time he never even attempted to bring me back.

That alone was answer enough for me.

It still is.

I step back from him, a retreat his keen gaze doesn't miss. "It's been nice seeing you, Nick." The lie sounds as tight as my smile feels when I look at him. "Enjoy the rest of the reception."

I hold out my hand the way I would to any other acquaintance or colleague. He takes it, but there is nothing casual about the way his fingers close around mine.

His grasp is firm and hot and certain. He holds my hand like a lover. Like a man who remembers as well as I do how often I've placed my trust in him and allowed him to lead me into every sensual place he wanted us to explore. After all the months we've been apart, he touches me like a man who's very much aware that he knows me better than anyone before him, or since.

His thumb brushes over the back of my hand. "Ready to run away from me already again?"

"I'm not running anywhere." I pull out of his loosened hold. "In case you haven't noticed, I've been gone for a long time, Nick. I've moved on."

"Have you?"

The question has an edge of challenge to it that makes me bristle. "What do you want from me? Don't you have anything better to do than trying to make me squirm?"

A world of meaning churns in his gaze, all of it dark and sensual. Arrogantly so. As intimate as a caress. "I don't want to make you uncomfortable, Avery."

"Good. Because I'm not going to do this with you. Not now. Not here."

"Then let's go somewhere else."

The suggestion makes me gape. "Leave with you? You can't be serious."

But he is. Dominic Baine offers nothing without careful deliberation. And when he sees something he wants, he pursues it with singular determination. I should know. That's how I ended up in his bed in the first place.

"I want you to go now, Nick."

I glance away from him because I have to. Because if I don't, I might be tempted to forget that this reception is important to me. And because if I stare any longer into those searing blue eyes, I might be tempted to forget about the fact that I came here with another man.

A good, decent man who's been nothing but kind to me in the two weeks we've been dating. I spot Brandon in the crowd finally. He's slowly making his way toward me, glasses of champagne in hand as he pauses here and there to converse and laugh with his colleagues from the university.

"Please, Nick. Just . . . go."

He follows my gaze into the throng, where Brandon now heads our way. Something dark flickers across Nick's face when he glances back at me. "Does he know about us?"

"No."

The denial feels like a betrayal of its own, despite the fact that Brandon and I have only been dating a short while. I haven't confided in him about anything, least of all the months I spent in Nick's bed. As for the rest of our history together, I have no intention of sharing that with Brandon or anyone else.

There's only one man who knows every secret and jagged facet of me and he's staring at me now with a look that's intimate and raw, seeing through me in the way he has from the very beginning.

As unsettling as Nick's scrutiny of me is, by the time Brandon arrives, his expression is shuttered into one of schooled indifference.

"Here you are!" Brandon grins as he hands me one of the flutes. "I've been looking for you for the past ten minutes. Sorry to keep you waiting on the bubbly. I ran into the dean at the bar and he started showing me pictures of his grandkids."

"It's all right," I murmur, taking the sweaty glass and watching as Brandon's attention flits to Nick. "Brandon, have you met Dominic Baine?"

"No, I haven't had the pleasure." He thrusts out his hand, pumping Nick's enthusiastically. "Brandon Snyder, sir. Art History department. It's wonderful to meet you, Mr. Baine. My colleagues and I are very grateful for your generous contributions to our fine institution over the years."

Nick's contributions. No wonder he was invited to the reception. I smile and sip my champagne as Brandon continues to effuse over Nick and the donations he's made to various departments of the university.

Before I realize it, I've drained my glass. Brandon notices it too. Chuckling, he draws me under his arm.

"Better take it easy on the bubbly, sweetheart. You need to be on stage for your speech in a few minutes."

"I'll be fine." I can't keep from looking at Nick as Brandon presses a kiss to my temple. It's a tender, yet possessive, move that shouldn't bother me, yet all I can feel is the measuring heat of Nick's gaze as he watches us together.

"We should head that way," Brandon reminds me. "Dean Witherspoon told me he'd like to say hello to you before everyone else starts gathering for his closing remarks."

"All right."

"If you'll excuse us," Brandon says, extending his hand to Nick once more. "Really great to meet you, sir. Now, if you don't mind, I'm going to have to steal my girl for a few minutes."

Nick merely grunts in response.

He doesn't look at me, but I burn under the intensity of his silence as Brandon places his hand at the small of my spine and leads me away.

3

"Avery Ross, you're a heartless bitch."

Jarred out of my concentration at the easel the next day, I glance up from my work in progress. "Excuse me?"

My studio mate Matt Hollis gives me a look that's anything but serious as he walks over to my work station. "You heard me, blondie. Heartless."

Since last summer, I've been sharing space with him and another friend, Lita Frasier, the tattooed, pierced, mixed-media sculptor who owns the small second-floor loft studio in East Harlem.

Matt holds a small collection of cleaned paintbrushes in his hand, which he uses to point at the gift-wrapped box that's been sitting on the edge of my work table since it arrived via courier that morning. "I realize it's your prezzie from the new man in your life, but when a friend gets a decadent box of hand-dipped French chocolates, it's customary for said friend to share the love with those less fortunate."

"What are you talking about? Of course, you can have some."

He tilts his chin low, rolling his eyes. "You haven't even opened the damn box yet."

He's right. I glance at the embossed gold paper with its red satin ribbon and bow, all still intact. There are few things in this world that I love more than chocolate, yet this particular box has been sitting untouched for more than an hour. As much as I appreciate Brandon's lavish gift, I can't think about France or knotted lengths of silken, scarlet fabric without thinking of *him*.

Not the man who sent this gift to me.

The one whose unexpected reappearance in my life last night has left me more rattled and confused than I care to admit, even to myself.

With Matt waiting eagerly for his chance to pounce on my chocolates, I unfasten the long red ribbon and tear the paper from the pretty box, holding it out to him. "Help yourself."

He reaches in and pops a truffle into his mouth. His eyes close as he chews.

"Oh, my God." His moan sounds practically orgasmic. "It's insane how good this is."

From across the studio, Lita swivels on her stool to face us. "I don't know how anyone's supposed to work around here with you two yapping and carrying on."

I laugh, because it's ironic she would complain about noise considering she prefers to work with a boom box blasting everything from Mozart to Metallica on any given day.

Lita gets up from the sculpture she's working on. The complicated tangle of metal wire and hammered steel has been her obsession for several weeks, a prototype for the piece that's recently been commissioned for the lobby of a high-profile corporate office in Brooklyn.

She saunters over in her usual black-on-black ensemble and combat boots. As of this morning, her pixie haircut is dyed platinum blonde with a dusting of cardinal red at the tips—the most traditional color combination I've seen on her in all these months. "Got any caramels in there?"

I shrug. "I think these two might be." I point and she takes one of them, biting into it.

"Ugh! Not even close." Her face scrunches, the little diamond stud in the side of her nose winking as she recoils. "What kind of animal puts frigging lavender in perfectly good chocolate?"

Matt chuckles and holds out his hand. "You're hopeless. Give it to me, heathen."

"Want to try a different one?" I ask.

"No thanks." She's still grimacing as she shakes her head and deposits her uneaten half into Matt's open palm. "Give me an old-fashioned candy bar any day. This fancy shit is not for me."

"Suit yourself," Matt says. He tosses back her lavender-infused reject, savoring it slowly before making grabby hands at me for another sample. He sets down his brushes and leans against my work table, indicating he plans to stay a while. "So, when are you going to spill some deets about the big reception last night? Did you have fun hobnobbing with the academic elite and all your adoring critics?"

I haven't told my friends at the studio that I ran into Nick. If they knew I spoke to him, I'd catch nothing but hell from both of them. They hate him because he hurt me, and they don't even know the half of it. Only my best friend, Tasha, knows the truth—and only because it was her doorstep I landed on after I fled back to New York from Paris.

I shrug as I meet Matt's questioning gaze. "It was okay."

"Just okay? Evidently the night ended more than okay if your date is following up with a two-hundred-dollar box of chocolates today."

I glance down, reflecting on how my encounter with Nick had shaded the rest of the evening. By the time I met the dean and made my little speech, he was gone. I know, because I couldn't keep my gaze from straying into the crowd the whole time, searching for his face. I could still hear his deep voice ringing in my head, my hand still heated from his touch.

I hadn't improved by the time Brandon took me home to my place. Instead of inviting him inside with me, I turned him away at the door with a lame excuse about a migraine and a chaste peck on the mouth. Not the first time, either. Yet rather than getting upset, Brandon sent me expensive chocolates with a sweet note and an invitation to dinner later in the week.

Matt pops another piece into his mouth, shivering in delight as he chews. "Damn, these are better than sex. Then again, maybe I just need to find a boyfriend like your hot nerd Professor. Do me a favor, Avery, when you decide to cut him loose, send him my way."

"What makes you think I'm going to cut Brandon

loose?"

Lita snickers while Matt rolls his eyes. "Please. Do we really need to have this conversation again?"

"What conversation?"

"What do you think is the longest you've dated anyone in the past twelve months?"

I don't like where he's going, but I lift my shoulder in a blasé shrug. "I have no idea."

"Eighteen days," he informs me. "Usually you don't even give a man half that amount of time before you kick his ass to the curb."

God, is he right? I've never kept track, but I doubt he's far off the mark.

"I guess I'm not very good at dating," I offer lamely.

"No kidding." He smirks, but there is affection in his eyes. "You're practically a monk, Avery. And why? With your looks and killer curves you could have your pick of any man in this city—and that was before you became the darling of the New York art world."

"I'm sure you must have a point in there somewhere."

"Yes, I have a point." He eyes me in scrutiny. "How long can you actually go without thinking about him? I'm going out on a limb here, but I'll bet it's somewhere between one hour and eighteen days."

"What does it matter?" He's not talking about Brandon or anyone else I've dated recently, and I don't pretend to misunderstand. "So, my social game sucks. That doesn't mean it has anything to do with Nick. I've moved on. End of story."

It's a familiar refrain, a mantra I've used to galvanize myself for the better part of the past year. Until last night, I had almost believed it.

Now, I'm not sure what I think.

Are you happy, Avery?

Nick's words come back at me for what isn't the first time. Am I happy? It's the one thing I haven't focused on since we broke up. The one question I've refused to ask myself because I know I don't want to hear the answer.

As always, he knows precisely how to cleave me closest to the bone.

"I'm over him," I insist, ignoring the dubious looks I'm getting from both of my friends.

They may not believe me, but I mean it with every fiber of my being.

I'm over him because I have to be.

Maybe happy will come later. Right now, I just need to survive. I need to protect my heart.

And that means staying as far away as possible from Dominic Baine.

4

Midtown traffic is a nightmare Friday night as Brandon and I, along with what seems like half the city's dating crowd, jockey to get somewhere for dinner. He parks his Volvo at a public garage, assuring me that we're less than two blocks from the restaurant.

"I hope you don't mind the walk." He casts me an uncertain glance. "I should've called about valet service at the restaurant or dropped you off first. Your feet must be killing you in those shoes."

"I'm fine." I step carefully in my new heels, doing my best to keep up with him while avoiding the grates and cracks in the concrete along the way. "I thought we were going to that steakhouse on Fifty-first?"

"Slight change of plans." He smiles, excitement

lighting his eyes. "Another opportunity came up a couple of days ago. I think you'll like it. The steakhouse is perfectly nice, but I wanted to surprise you with something different tonight."

"All right." I don't tell him that I hate surprises. Or, rather, I had hated them, before I met Nick. He taught me to enjoy a lot of things I never dreamed I would. Including a few that would probably light mild-mannered Brandon's hair on fire. "How much farther is it?"

"We're almost there." He points up ahead of us, where a well-dressed crowd spills out to the sidewalk in front of a warmly lit restaurant. The buzz of excitement around the place is palpable even before we near it.

"Looks like a popular place."

He grins. "Tonight's the Grand Opening. One of my colleagues in the history department scored reservations three months ago, but he and his wife have been out all week with that respiratory thing that's going around. Lucky us, he gave the reservation to me."

He holds his arm out, guiding me ahead of him as we step past the other people on our way to the doors. A pair of stylized, interlocking initials—a G and a C—gleam in hammered steel at the center of the polished glass.

My feet slow to a halt as I realize where we are. "This is Gavin Castille's new restaurant."

"Yes, it is." Brandon beams at me, reaching for the door. "Don't look so worried. I hear his food is outstanding, unlike some of the other celebrity chefs out there."

It's not the food that gives me pause. I know firsthand that the Australian chef creates culinary masterpieces. He also happens to be a close friend of Nick's.

"Are you disappointed?" Brandon's eager look turns confused, crestfallen. "Because if you'd rather go somewhere else—"

"No, of course not." After all, there's no reason I shouldn't enjoy dinner at what's clearly one of the hottest new places in the city. I'm not going to let thoughts of Nick dampen my evening with Brandon. Especially when he's trying so hard to please me.

Some of my resolve fades as we enter the restaurant and I see Gavin personally greeting his Grand Opening patrons. Like the consummate host he is, the handsome Aussie with the easy smile and beachy blond mane of hair takes a moment to speak with each person as they arrive and report in at the host stand. There are two couples ahead of Brandon and me, but I don't miss the brief flick of Gavin's eyes in my direction.

He doesn't seem surprised to see me without Nick, although I'm sure by now he's well aware that his friend and I are no longer seeing each other. I cringe to think Gavin might also be aware of the reasons why.

Had Nick confided in him about how he'd used me? God, had Gavin known all along what he'd done—even that night when he'd shown up and prepared a private gourmet dinner for us at Nick's request?

My cheeks warm to recall it, particularly the dessert of strawberries and cream and chocolate sauce, all of which Nick served to me later that evening while I was blindfolded and undressed, my hands tied at my back with a long string of pearls.

When it's our turn to meet Gavin, he gives me no reason to feel uncomfortable. In fact, he introduces himself as though it's the first time he's ever seen me. For my benefit or my date's? I can't be sure, but I'm grateful nonetheless.

He shakes Brandon's hand, then clasps mine in a brief, warm grasp. "Good evening. Welcome to GC."

"Thank you." I hold his pale green gaze without saying anything more, and he shrewdly picks up on my awkwardness. I wonder if he shares it, because he spends only a moment with us before motioning one of the hostesses over to him.

"Shelly, please seat this young lady and the gentleman in the library room."

Brandon holds up his hand in question. "Actually, I believe the reservation I have is for the gallery room."

"You just got an upgrade, mate." Gavin's wink and broad, dimpled smile are pure charm. "I promise, you'll love your table in the library even more."

Brandon chuckles. "Well, in that case, thank you."

"My pleasure," Gavin says, his glance lingering on mine for just a second longer as a party of four excitedly comes up to meet him. He nods to me. "Enjoy your evening, both of you."

The hostess holds two large, leather-covered menus in her arms. "This way, please."

We walk behind her as she leads us through the bustling restaurant. The layout is unique, especially for Manhattan. Rather than a sleek or fussy open-concept fishbowl, Gavin's new restaurant is comprised of cozy dining rooms with exposed brick, rug-covered plank-wood floors, white stucco walls and heavy beamed ceilings.

It's intimate and elegant, yet warmly inviting. But there's no question that it's also the place to be and be seen, especially tonight. The restaurant is filled with important looking people, couples on Friday night dates as well as larger groups. In one crowded dining room, tables surround a pianist playing light chamber music on a gleaming baby grand. Front and center, I notice the city's mayor, Don Holbrook, holding court with his wife at a table for six. I've never met the mayor, but nearly a year ago I attended one of his fundraising galas.

With Nick, of course.

I groan inwardly at the memory. Is there anywhere I can go in this city without being reminded of him at every turn?

Brandon gently takes my hand as the hostess escorts us further into the restaurant. "What do you think? Do you like it so far?"

I nod. "It's wonderful, and the food smells amazing."

"Only the best for my girl," he says, giving my fingers a little squeeze.

We are shown to one of half a dozen tables situated in a romantic room lined with floor-to-ceiling polished cherry bookcases. Hundreds upon hundreds of antique books fill the beautiful shelves. Their supple leather spines and gold-leaf lettering twinkle in the low light from the sconces on the walls and the enormous chandelier that hangs down from an ornate ceiling medallion in the center of the room.

"Wow." I can't hold back my pleasure as I drink in every detail.

Brandon seems equally impressed. He grins at the hostess as she seats us and presents us with our menus. "Please let the chef know that I definitely approve of the seating change."

Her smile is placid. "He will be happy to hear it, I'm sure. Your server will be with you momentarily. Bon appétit."

We aren't left waiting long. Despite the full house, Gavin's staff are prompt, polite, and effortlessly professional. Our waiter takes our drink order and another server brings fresh bread and seasoned oil. Others carry trays laden with cocktails, food, and sumptuous desserts, everyone moving in a symphony of polished grace and skill.

Brandon's head swivels with each new culinary creation that passes by. "My word, did you see that rack of lamb? If the food is as good as it looks, we're in for a real treat tonight."

"Yes, we are," I agree, taking a sip of my wine.

"You know, Castille's got another place on the Upper East Side. Maybe we should go check that one out too."

"Sure. I'd like that." I nod as I break off a small piece of bread and dip it into the little plate of oil and herbs.

I've been to Gavin's other restaurant before, although I doubt Brandon would care to hear about that any more than he'd want to know about any of my other experiences with Nick. God, what does it say about me that I can't think of a single instance when I was able to resist that man?

He had a way of turning every moment into something heated and dangerous, something too powerful to be denied.

Seeing him at the university gallery reception a few nights ago only drove that fact home with renewed clarity. As hard as I've tried to put our encounter out of my mind all week, there is a part of me that wonders what would have happened if I'd taken Nick up on his suggestion that we go somewhere to talk.

Not that I have to wonder.

Too many heated dreams in the nights since have filled in all of the blanks.

Brandon hails our waiter with a little wave of his hand. "Any chance I could get some butter for the bread?"

A perfunctory nod. "Of course, sir."

"Thanks, appreciate it," he says, then lowers his voice when we're alone again. "You'd think a swanky place like this would know to bring butter to the table too."

He's not watching where his hand is, and as he reaches for the bread basket, the cuff of his sport coat catches on his long-stemmed wineglass. It tips before either of us can react, spilling merlot across the white table linens and onto my lap.

"Oh, no!" He pops out of his chair and starts to move toward me with his napkin in hand. "Avery, I'm sorry."

"It's all right," I say, feeling more awkward about the stares we're drawing than the accident itself. "Fortunately, my dress is a dark color. It'll be fine."

He frowns, vigorously shaking his head. "I'm such a clod. Let me help you—"

"No, it's okay, really." I stand up, the scent of wine clinging to me. "I, ah, I think I'll go find the ladies' room and clean up."

He looks mortified, still fussing and apologizing as I extricate myself from our table to look for the restroom. The trek takes me deeper into the restaurant, the sounds of soft music and mingled conversations filtering out from all directions.

As I walk, I pass an intimate dining room sporting a carved limestone fireplace at one end and walls adorned with a variety of interesting art. Dozens of creative vignettes of framed paintings and striking photography. Cornice shelves showcasing unusual sculpture and rustic carvings that seem to be a celebration of art from all over the world.

The gallery room, obviously.

The art draws my gaze as I stroll by. If my thighs weren't damp and the front of my dress reeking of spilled wine, I'd be tempted to slow down or even drift inside the room to take a closer look.

I'm not sure what pulls my attention away from the art and into one cozy corner of the room. But once I glance that way, I don't see anything else.

It's Nick.

And he's not alone.

The blonde woman seated across from him is beautiful, dazzling, in fact. She's dressed in a low-backed dress and red-soled stilettos. Long, elegant fingers hold the stem of her wineglass as she leans forward, speaking animatedly to Nick, her adoring eyes riveted on him. He says something and she laughs, placing her hand over the top of his.

My breath seizes in my lungs.

No wonder Gavin made sure to seat Brandon and me in another room. He knew Nick was here too. With someone else. Someone whose regal appearance and easy grace exude old-money wealth and sophistication.

Someone who looks like she belongs in his world, much more than I ever could be, no matter how successful I've become in the time since we've been apart.

Is he using her too? Another acquisition to add to his long list of conquests? I'm sure I don't want to know.

I glance away and keep walking, dreading the possibility that he might notice me too. Of course, he doesn't. He's too focused on the new woman across from him.

I can only be grateful for that small mercy.

I'm sure as hell not ready to face him like this, with Brandon's merlot all over me and Nick with a stunning date on his arm.

To my relief, a departing group of diners heads toward me from the opposite end of the walkway. I skirt the far edge of them, putting their party between me and Nick's line of vision as I step quickly past the gallery dining room.

As soon as I'm through the swinging door of the ladies' room, I sag against the wall and let go of the air that's trapped in my lungs.

Breathe, Avery. Just breathe. God, it's not easy to do.

He's here. After a year of taking every step possible to avoid him, now, he's just in the other room. Enjoying a romantic dinner with another woman.

I should be relieved. Hell, I should be overjoyed that he's enjoying a romantic dinner with another woman after trying to play me again the other night at the reception. That pitiful part of me that has been tethered to what we had, waiting for Nick to either come around and beg me for forgiveness or confirm once and for all that nothing we shared was real has just been given its freedom.

So, why do the backs of my eyes sting with hot tears as I head over to the sink and begin to clean the spilled wine from my dress?

Why does my reflection look so miserable when I should be elated to finally have some closure?

Because, apparently, getting my heart broken by Dominic Baine has taught me nothing.

Am I really so weak? Or is his hold on me simply that strong, even after all this time, after all the lies and the anger and the pain?

The door swings open and an elderly woman enters, giving me a sympathetic glance as I dab at the front of my dress with a paper towel. I've done about all I can to get the wine out, but I linger in the restroom, knowing damn well I'm stalling.

The older woman joins me at the trio of sinks to wash her hands. "I've cried over a few ruined dresses in my day," she says, smiling kindly at me in the mirror. "You should try some soda water on that, dear. Works like a charm."

I nod and murmur my thanks, waiting until she's left before I toss my dampened paper towels into the trash. Then, girding myself for the gauntlet that will take me past Nick and his date once more, I exit and head back to rejoin Brandon.

I don't know whether to be relieved or disappointed to see that Nick and his companion are gone by the time I pass the gallery room. Their table is being bussed, already making room for other diners.

I assure myself I'm not the least bit curious where they've gone. Not the least bit stung to imagine him taking her back to his penthouse for a night of pleasures I can imagine all too easily.

"Everything okay?" Brandon reaches for my hand after I slip back into my seat at our table.

I nod, calling upon a smile that aches more than I care to acknowledge. "Yes. Everything's just fine."

5

The next afternoon, I'm seated at the bar at Vendange, the Madison Avenue restaurant where I used to work with my best friend, Tasha. Although the place is usually packed to capacity with bankers, traders, and other corporate types day and night during the week, the Saturday lunch crowd leans more toward power shoppers, sightseers, and well-heeled couples out to explore the city.

Tasha's been managing the restaurant for more than a year now, and somehow she makes it look easy. I can't help but feel a sense of pride as I watch her handle customers and staff with equal parts smooth professionalism and exuberant charm. Vendange had been popular enough when I worked behind the bar, but Tasha's management of the hotspot has taken its success to a whole new level.

She's smiling as she breaks away from a table of happy customers and finally heads my way, pausing to place an order with the bartender. "Caleb, will you pour me a glass of that new Malbec that just came in, please?"

While he nods and pivots away to fetch the drink, she comes over and envelops me in a warm hug. "Hey, you! Sorry to leave you sitting over here for so long. We've been going nonstop since the doors opened today."

"I see that. Things are going well."

"We're having a record month," she says, hooking some of her soft brown spiral curls behind her ear as she releases me. Her cheeks are bright, her gorgeous doe eyes dancing as she hops onto the recently vacated stool beside me. "At this rate, I'm going to have to expand the kitchen staff again and hire a few more servers. Not to mention I'm gonna need an assistant manager sooner than later."

I laugh, my brows lifting in surprise. "An assistant manager for my best friend, the ultimate boss lady? I'm shocked."

"Yeah, well, not like I have much choice." She shrugs, her grin widening. "I'm pregnant."

"Tasha! Oh, my God, that's amazing news."

"I know, right? My little Zoe's going to be a big sister." She starts giggling, and then I'm laughing along with her, my heart leaping at the pure joy I see in her face. No wonder she seems to be glowing today. Although she's being careful to keep her voice quiet, I can see that she's practically bursting with excitement.

"How long have you known? I saw you and Tony last week and you didn't say anything."

"I wasn't sure. I mean, had a feeling I might be knocked up, but I just took the test this morning to confirm it. We're not going to officially announce for a little while yet, just to be sure. You're the first one to know, aside from Tony and his mom, of course."

"Congratulations. I'm so happy for you." I squeeze her hands, feeling elated and yet a tiny bit envious.

When I was seeing Nick, she used to tease me about all of the extravagant places we went, all the romantic things we did. She would jokingly contrast her lifestyle to mine, as if the fantasy I was living in Nick's Park Avenue penthouse was somehow leagues away from anything she would ever have.

Even before my happiness with Nick came crashing down around me, I knew that what Tasha had with Tony was pretty close to perfect.

"Here's your wine, Tasha." The bartender sets the glass down in front of her. When he moves on to greet a new customer, I tilt my head at her in question.

She rolls her eyes. "It's for you. Obviously, it's off limits for me now." She slides the glass next to the iced tea I've been nursing since I arrived. "I'm thinking about adding this to our regular list. You're so good with wine, I'd love your opinion on it first." A small frown creases her forehead. "And unless I miss my guess, it looks like you could use something a little stronger than what you're drinking today."

I won't argue that. She studies me as I tilt the glass to my lips and taste the smooth red wine.

"How'd the reception go on Friday? You and Blandon have a nice time with all of his stuffy university chums?"

"Brandon," I say, slanting a wry glance at her. "The

reception was great. I must've talked with half a dozen art magazines who wanted interviews and photos, and I went home with business cards from two of the best galleries in the city. As for Brandon's colleagues, they weren't stuffy at all. They were wonderful. He even introduced me to the dean."

Tasha's eyes stay rooted on me as I pause my ramble to take another drink of wine. "Sounds amazing, Ave. So, what am I missing?"

"Nick was there."

"What?" Her outburst turns several heads at the bar. She leans in closer, dropping her volume to a private level. "What the hell was he doing there?"

I purse my lips. "He had an invitation, just like everyone else," I say, recalling his slightly annoyed tone when I asked him the same thing that night. "Apparently, Nick's been generous with donations to the university over the years. Brandon practically fell all over himself with praise when I introduced them."

"Awkward."

"A bit," I agree. "Nick actually had the nerve to ask me to leave the party with him."

Tasha gapes. "In front of the professor?"

"No. Before that. We bumped into each other while Brandon was circulating. I don't think Nick was any happier than I was to find out we were in the same place, but that didn't stop him from acting like there was still something between us. When I told him I didn't want to talk to him anymore, especially considering where we were, he suggested we leave together."

"Interesting."

"If by *interesting* you mean arrogant, then yeah. He was. Which is typical of him."

Tasha shrugs. "I don't suppose he got where he is in life by being shy."

"No, he got there by looking out for himself and taking whatever he wants." I narrow my eyes at her as I lift the wineglass to my lips. "Whose side are you on, anyway?"

She holds up her hands in surrender. "Just saying."

Although it would be a stretch to say that Tasha and Nick were friends, she is familiar with the way he operates in business at least. He's the reason she's in charge at Vendange and no longer working behind the bar for the jerk who used to manage the place.

Nick bought the restaurant after we'd been seeing each other for several months. If he hadn't promptly sold it after our breakup, jettisoning it almost as swiftly as he seemed to purge me from his life, Tasha had been determined to quit in solidarity with me.

I'm glad it didn't come to that because it's clear how much she loves her job. She's invested more than just her time into Vendange. Her personal touches in the restaurant are evident in everything from the upscale clothing style and strong morale of the staff to the innovative menu items and creative wine selections.

For Nick's part, he seemed to understand that too. One of the conditions he placed on the sale was that Tasha was to remain at the helm.

I salute her with my half-empty glass. "This Malbec is excellent, by the way. Is it from Argentina?"

"France," she says, giving a dismissive wave of her hand. "Forget the wine. Tell me more about the party. Aside from being as arrogant as ever, how'd Nick look?"

"Good." I see no point in trying to deny it. Not with her. I let go of a resigned sigh. "He looked ridiculously good."

"Ah, fuck. Of course, he did."

Tasha is well aware of how physical and consuming my attraction to him was. I don't want to admit that his effect on my senses is still as powerful as ever, but she'd never believe it if I pretended otherwise.

"If anything, he's only gotten better looking," I add, sipping my wine. "Evidently, single life has been good for him."

"You don't know that."

"No? Well, he looked damn good last night, too, when I was with Brandon at Gavin Castille's new restaurant and saw Nick there having an intimate dinner with a gorgeous blonde."

Just saying it stings more than I want it to. I want to be over him. I want him to be relegated to my past, where I can better cope with his absence and all of the hurt that goes along with it.

Seeing him at the party tore at the edges of too many of those wounds again. Seeing him on a date with another woman just a couple of nights later ripped a piece of me wide open.

I'm not over him yet. I probably never will be. I gave him too much of me, things I won't ever be able to give anyone else.

The one thing neither of us seemed capable of truly giving each other was honesty.

Tasha winces as I take another swig of the Malbec, a bigger one this time. "What happened after you saw them?"

"Nothing. I was on my way to the restroom. They were gone by the time I came out."

"Did he see you?"

"I don't think so. God, I hope not."

Her silence stretches for a long moment. "What about Brandon?"

"What about him?"

"Does he know you're still in love with Nick? For that matter, did any of the other handful of guys you've briefly dated in the past year know that?"

I stare at her, wishing I could balk at the suggestion. If it were anyone else I would.

"I don't know what I feel for Nick besides hurt and betrayed and confused. Am I over him? No. But I sure as hell don't want to be in love with him. You should understand that better than anyone."

She nods slowly, no doubt recalling the mess I was during those first weeks back in the city. She and Tony took me in when I had nowhere else to go, making room for me in their already crowded home as though I were family. She saw me through the crying jags and the anger, and she helped pushed me back into my art as a means of off-loading all of my pain into something more productive.

"Yeah, Avery, I do understand. And I hate the bastard for how he hurt you. But how I feel about him doesn't really matter. You need to figure out what he means to you. Maybe he needs to tell you what you mean to him too."

I scoff. "I got that answer loud and clear in Paris, and in the twelve months since. All I was to him was an object to be acquired. He manipulated every aspect of my life—my job, my home, *everything*—until the only path I had left was the one that would lead me straight to him. I mean, how cold do you have to be to do that to someone? How would I ever forgive him for that?"

"Maybe you should ask him that question, not me." Her eyes turn soft, sympathetic. "Call him, Avery. Have the talk you both have been avoiding for the past year."

"No way. Not happening." I down the remainder of the wine and set the glass on the bar. "I have no interest in letting him back into my life again. I can't do it, Tasha."

She arches a brow at me. "Then skip the talk and just go fuck him like you want to do. Get him out of your system and get some closure, if that's possible. It'd serve him right to be the one getting screwed over for a change."

"Oh, my God." I gape at her because she's clearly lost her mind to even suggest it. "You give really terrible advice sometimes, you know that?"

She grins, entirely without shame. "Hey, I'm just trying to help. You've told me yourself that you haven't gone to bed with anyone since him, and that's a damn long time for a woman to go without. Besides, nothing wrong with some good old-fashioned revenge sex— even if you gotta get it from him."

I shake my head, appalled. Not only at her, but at myself for the way my body reacts to the idea of sleeping with Nick again, even under the dubious conditions Tasha's proposing.

Despite my intellect's best efforts to shut down even the thought of it, desire prickles inside me. Like a living current of electricity, it slides through my veins slick and hot and intense, fueled by the knowledge of how good Nick and I were together.

We were better than good together. He was the best lover I ever had, and no matter how badly things ended, I know he was every bit as caught up in me. Seeing him the other night at the reception almost had me believing that he might still be.

Almost.

Fortunately, my pride proved stronger than any weakness I apparently continue to have where he's concerned. I don't want to think about how idiotic I would feel today if I had let our encounter escalate at the reception, or, much worse, had I been foolish enough to let him persuade me into leaving with him, even just to talk.

Tasha studies me as I run my thumb along the rim of the empty wineglass, my thoughts conflicted and my heart pounding heavily in my breast. She reaches out, placing her hand gently on my forearm, her brown eyes soft with concern.

"Never mind all that shit I said just now. You're right, it's terrible advice. I was only trying to make you laugh." I offer her a wan smile and she chortles. "Good lord, that bad, huh?"

"Don't worry about it. I love you anyway."

"Love you too." She blows out a slow sigh, her gaze dropping to her watch. "I guess I should get back to work."

I nod. "Sure, okay. I want to head over to the studio for a while."

If there's one thing I can count on to clear my head and set me back to rights, it's sitting in front of my easel with a paintbrush in hand. I slide off the barstool and Tasha follows, hopping down off hers to embrace me in another warm hug.

She steps back, pointing her finger at me. "If you're free on Sunday, Tony's mom is making her famous chicken cacciatore. Wanna come? You know it's to die for."

I can't remember the last home-cooked meal I've had, and Tasha's mother-in-law makes some of the best. My stomach practically growls in agreement. "I'd love to. Thanks."

"Great. Inez will be glad to see you at the table with us again. Zoe too. She misses her Auntie Avery."

"I can't wait to be there."

We say our goodbyes and I'm smiling with anticipation as I head out the door to the sunny summer afternoon outside. I see the sleek black BMW M6 standing at the curb in front of me, but at first it seems like a mirage. A trick of this vast city, where it isn't unusual to see vehicles worth many hundreds of thousands of dollars idling at traffic lights or speeding along the gridwork of boulevards.

But this particular vehicle is one I've been inside numerous times, one I know all too well.

The driver's side door opens, and my feet slow beneath me as I watch Dominic Baine step out. He's not dressed in his business armor of a bespoke suit and tie today, but even sporting a basic white T-shirt and well-worn jeans, he still carries himself like a man who could—and probably does—own a healthy chunk of the bustling city that surrounds him.

He says nothing, merely watches me from over the gleaming roof of the car.

All the air in my lungs flees as I realize this is no chance meeting like the other two times I've seen him in the past week.

No, he's come to Vendange deliberately, possibly even been waiting outside for some time. The way he's looking at me as he waits for my acknowledgment leaves no doubt about that.

He's here right now for one reason.

Me.

6

Avery's bright smile fades the moment her eyes land on me.

Whatever joy she'd been feeling is gone in an instant, snuffed out and cold. For the brief second she pauses on the sidewalk outside Vendange, all I see in her beautiful face is pain and confusion, suspicion.

I shouldn't be surprised. After all, I'm the one who's done this to her.

Not only that morning in Paris, but more recently too.

She doesn't even attempt to conceal her displeasure as she turns away from me without so much as a word. She starts heading up the sidewalk in the opposite direction of me.

"Avery, wait."

Her pace doesn't slow at all. I bite off a curse as I cut the M6's engine and close the door. There's no parking on this section of the street, but the last thing I'm worried about is a paltry ticket or a tow. Rounding the front of the vehicle, I catch up to her in a few determined strides.

"Avery." I step ahead, then turn to face her. My body blocks her immediate path, the only thing that seems to make her stop. "Goddamn it, don't go."

My voice sounds too raw, enough to make her gaze snap up to mine in alarm. I rein it in with a scowl. It's astonishing how quickly she can rattle my self-control. Then again, it shouldn't surprise me. This woman has twisted me into knots from the first moment I laid eyes on her.

Gritting my teeth against the urge to physically hold her in place, I try again. "Don't run from me. Please."

She doesn't try to, but she glares in defiance, her lips flattened into a tight line. "What are you trying to do, Nick?"

"I want to talk to you."

A thin scoff escapes her. "I can't imagine why."

"I think you can."

She's pissed off, and as much as I hate being the target of her loathing, I can't help wondering if last night at Gavin's restaurant has anything to do with it. The question kept me awake for hours after I left the place. More than once, I had keys in hand, half-tempted to seek her out no matter the time. Instead, after pacing the penthouse like a caged animal until the sun rose, I wasn't about to go the entire day without seeing her.

"How did you know where to find me?" There is challenge in her voice, and in the narrowed stare that searches my gaze. "Don't try to tell me you just happened to be in the neighborhood."

"No. I wasn't." At my admission, she folds her arms, her expression perturbed but far from shocked. "I wanted to see you. I drove by your place in Forest Hills this morning, but you were already out. I checked for you at the studio in Harlem too. Lita said she didn't know where you were—right before she told me to go to hell and slammed the door in my face."

Avery's stare remains stubbornly militant. "Good to know someone's got my back."

I don't doubt that all of her friends despise me. They have every right to. They're protective of her, the way people who care for one another are supposed to be. They're loyal and true. All the things I wanted to be for Avery, *tried to be,* but failed.

It's too late to take anything back. I can't undo any of it. The wounded look on her face warns me not to even try, but I've never been good at taking direction.

"Since you weren't anywhere else I looked, I assumed you might be with Tasha at Vendange."

She exhales sharply. "You assume a lot. What if I was on a date?" She tosses the suggestion out at me like a volley shot over my bow. "Would you have come after me there too?"

I don't reply because there is no need. She can probably read the answer in my hot, unflinching stare. "Fortunately for both of us, you aren't on a date."

As she frowns up at me, I consider the eager, ruddy-faced art history professor who'd been her escort at the university reception earlier this week. Although I hadn't known anything about the congenial bastard until that night, I am considerably more informed now.

Brandon Snyder is a hardworking, decent man from a solid, middle-class family upstate. Stellar academic and public records. Not a single blemish on his character anywhere to be found.

Because damn it, I've looked.

After realizing he was dating Avery, I made it my next day's mission to unearth every piece of data I could find on him.

In the end, all I found was a man far better suited for her than I ever could be.

Hell, if I'm keeping score, there are countless men in this city who deserve Avery more than I do. But not any one of them will ever love her the way I did . . . the way I still do.

They'll never please her the same way.

They'll never hurt her so deeply, either.

I lift my hand before I realize what I'm doing, needing to touch her. She steps back as if I mean to strike her instead of caress her.

"No. Don't." A firm shake of her head sends her loose blonde hair sifting around her shoulders. "You don't get to do that anymore, Nick. You don't have the right. Not that you ever did."

"I suppose I deserve that."

"And then some."

Apparently, she's had enough. She moves to the right as if to step around me. I counter, cutting off her escape. "Have you eaten yet?"

"What?"

"Lunch. I'm starving, and there's no point in standing here trying to have a conversation in the middle of the sidewalk. So, what do you say? Let's go somewhere more private and talk."

"Let me guess," she replies, sarcasm lacing every syllable. "Somewhere private as in back to your place? Maybe you think we should have this conversation in your bed?"

Christ. It wasn't my intention to bring her home with me today, but my cock and everything else male in me responds with swift approval. "I'm definitely not opposed to the idea."

The frown creasing her forehead deepens. "You're unbelievable. If you want to share a meal and some conversation with someone—or anything else—I'm sure you have plenty of other options available to you. In fact, why don't you start with the blonde you had dinner with last night?"

I scowl, if only to cover the satisfaction I feel in seeing Avery's jealousy spike even after all this time. Even after everything that stands between us. "You mean Simone? What do you know about her?"

She scoffs under her breath. "I guess I should thank you for not attempting to lie to my face about it. I saw you with her at Gavin's restaurant, not that I care. You're free to fuck whoever you want. It doesn't matter to me."

"Really?" I study her, reacquainting myself with every nuance of her face, every emotion that plays across her delicate features no matter how hard she tries to conceal it from me. It stung her to see me with another woman. It still does, all these hours later.

Just as it burned me to think of her with another man.

"As I recall it, you were with someone at GC last night too."

"So, you did see me." She says it with resignation, as if she'd be more shocked if I hadn't noticed her presence inside the crowded restaurant. Perhaps even disappointed.

The fact is, I would sense this woman anywhere. There isn't a place I've gone in this city where I haven't been acutely, painfully aware of her.

I am drawn to her now as I have been from the beginning, even though I know I've forfeited the right to act on it.

No, as she said only a few moments ago, I never had that right.

Regardless, I see no reason to play games with Avery. I've done enough of that already. And I know that if she believes she's right—that I screwed the woman she saw me having dinner with just a couple of nights after I asked Avery to leave her art event with me—our conversation would end right here.

"Simone Emmons lost her husband last month."

Avery tilts her head, far from convinced. "She didn't look the part of a grieving widow to me. Especially when she was pawing at you across the table and batting her lashes."

I shrug, unable to offer any defense for my dinner companion. "Simone is a flirtatious woman who married a wealthy man old enough to be her grandfather. She's also my newest client. At dinner last night, she agreed to sell one of her deceased husband's companies to me."

Avery snorts. "I'll bet she did. I'll bet you were one hard negotiator too."

"It was just business, and it went no further than dinner." I pause as a cluster of pedestrians moves past us on the concrete. "Do you really want to talk about Simone Emmons?"

"No." I see some of her suspicion diffuse, but not

enough to persuade her to stay. "I don't want to talk about anything with you, Nick. I'm on my way to the studio. Or, rather, I would be if you weren't standing in my way."

"Let me drive you there."

"No, thanks." Something brittle flashes in her gaze. "I don't accept rides from people I don't know."

It's a low blow, lower than anything else she's said to me, but a deserved one. If I were a better man, I'd let her aptly delivered jab stick and head back to my car alone. For the past year I've managed to resist a confrontation like this, but after seeing her a few nights ago she's all I've been able to think about.

I have things to say to her.

Things I should have said back in Paris or months before.

There are things she needs to know. Things she needs to see. Ugly things that may make her hate me even more. Or worse, pity me.

"All right, Avery. Then walk with me for a while. If you decide you still don't know me, then I'll escort you to the nearest subway station and I'll go. You'll never see me again."

She stares at me, a trace of confusion in her searching gaze. I see doubt there too. When she speaks, her voice is quiet, hesitant. "You really mean that?"

Fuck, do I? As difficult as it would be to keep a promise like that, I know I owe her the choice. The choice I didn't give her before. I owe her the truth . . . and the why.

"Yes, Avery. I mean it. You have my word."

For a long while, she says nothing. Doesn't so much as blink as she weighs my promise in unbearable silence.

She can break me right here and now, but I wonder if she truly understands her power. Watching her leave the first time was hard enough. Knowing how deeply I'd hurt her was a torment that's eaten at me like a cancer ever since.

She doesn't trust me. She doesn't believe that I can be held to any promises, nor should she. But I would do this for her now. Not only because I know it's the best thing for her, but because I also know the shame that's waiting at the end of the path I'm asking her to walk with me.

I haven't opened that door since the moment Avery entered my life.

I'm not at all certain I want to do it now.

She watches me too closely, already far too aware of the fissures in my soul.

"Okay, Nick," she says softly. "Lead the way."

7

Nick leaves his BMW disregarded at the curb outside Vendange as we begin walking.

I'd been mentally commending myself for holding my ground and refusing to make the mistake of being alone with him, but even amid the rush and bustle of Manhattan and its constantly moving sea of humanity, the only thing I'm truly aware of is him.

My senses stir as we walk side by side on the concrete, our arms not quite brushing against each other as clusters of pedestrians ebb and flow around us. I know the scent and the feel and the taste of every inch of his perfectly honed body, no matter how desperately I want to pretend I don't.

He smells amazing. Spicy and warm, intoxicatingly masculine, something that can't be bought or manufactured, but is his alone. Everything female in me wants to lean in to that scent, to carry it on my skin like a brand. Especially when I watch other women glance at him in open interest as we pass them on the street.

"How's Tasha doing?"

The casual question catches me off guard. I know Nick's got an agenda for this conversation, and the fact that he's starting it with small talk only makes my nerves jangle even more than they were already.

"She's fine." I keep Tasha's baby news to myself, even though it takes some effort not to share it with Nick. Calling him a stranger back at the curb was easier than treating him like one when he's walking so close to me I can focus on little else. "Tasha's doing great. She's amazing. I'm so proud of everything she's done with Vendange."

Nick grunts in acknowledgment. "The new owner couldn't be more pleased, either. And the bastard ought to be. He got the restaurant for a song and it's nearly doubled in business in the past several months."

Thinking about how quickly he'd divested himself of the business—along with me—I can't help the bite in my reply. "I'm so sorry for your loss, Nick. I know how you love to win."

He shrugs. "Yeah, well. I'll get over it."

"I'm sure you will. I'm sure you've already moved on to bigger and better things. You're pretty good at that."

The look he swivels on me is penetratingly intense. "Is that what you think?"

"It's what I know, Nick."

"Do you." It's not a question, more a challenge. But just because his dinner date last night was a client doesn't mean there haven't been other women. With Nick's considerable appetite when it comes to sex, I don't doubt that he's got a string of available women at his beck and call in a moment's notice. "And what about you, Avery? Has moving on without me been easy for you?"

"It sure as hell should be. I was taught by a master." I give him a pointed glance. "No pun intended."

His brow quirks, sin playing at the edges of his sensual mouth. But there is no playfulness in the stare that holds steady on me as we near the traffic light at the end of the block. "Are you saying it hasn't been easy, or that you haven't moved on? Because either way, I think your smitten Professor Snyder would be dismayed to hear that."

"This isn't about Brandon, so you can leave him out of the picture."

"I don't think he's in the picture at all. If he was, you'd have left me high and dry at the curb back there."

I bark a laugh. "God, you're arrogant. If I thought you knew how to take no for an answer, I would have left you at the curb." I shoot him a sidelong glance. "I still should."

His smile is subtle, more amused than threatened. "This way."

For the briefest second I feel the heat of his palm hovering at the small of my back as we round the corner off Madison, but Nick doesn't touch me. His warmth is there and gone so quickly I might have imagined it, leaving me both disappointed and relieved. I fold my arms as we walk for a while in silence, if only to avoid any more inadvertent contact with him. My senses are hyperaware enough as it is. I don't need any tactile reminders of how good it feels to touch him or feel his touch on me.

We pass shops and boutique hotels and eateries, the sidewalk thickening with pedestrians as we near the corner of broad, busy Fifth Avenue. Waiting at the traffic light, a mother holds the hand of her young daughter and points toward the Public Library across the street with its pair of majestic marble lions flanking the grand entrance. I can't help but smile at the excitement in the child's face as Nick and I step past them. He notices my distraction too.

"I trust your mother is in good health and doing well?"

My gaze snaps to him, although it's not the strangest question he could ask. He knows more about my mom than most people. Things I confided in him when we were together. Things he eventually learned in spite of my efforts to hold on to my mom's secrets and my own.

And now I have to wonder . . .

"The parole board finally decided to let her go about eight months ago. A new chairman was appointed and Mom's case got fast-tracked for another review." Since he doesn't react with anything more than a slight nod, my suspicions about her abrupt release from prison in Pennsylvania after a decade of little hope are all but confirmed. "You had something to do with it?"

He gives a vague shrug as we continue to walk. "As luck would have it, Beck went to law school with the state's Attorney General."

Beck being Andrew Beckham, Nick's personal lawyer and good friend. I've met the handsome African-American a few times, enough to have recognized there is probably no one Nick trusts more as a colleague or a confidant.

"There may have been some conversations on the golf course between the AG and the Governor about the need for fresh eyes on the parole board," Nick says. "Fortunately, it didn't take too much convincing that your mother is no danger to society any more now than she was ten years ago."

I know I'm gaping, but I can hardly help it. Even though Nick once told me he'd be willing to leverage his connections and assets to assist my mom with her legal problems, I can't believe he actually followed through with it. Not only because I forbade him to interfere in my life or hers in order to protect the awful secret that she and I shared.

I hadn't wanted Nick to know what lies I'd buried in my past. I wanted the abuse I'd suffered to stay behind me, along with the truth about my stepfather's murder and the fact that my mother had sacrificed so much— including her freedom—in order to protect me.

But Nick did find out. And when those secrets threatened to explode in my face with the reappearance of my stepbrother, Rodney Coyle, and his threats against my mother and me, Nick was the one who stopped him. He saved my life, I have no doubt.

And now I realize he's given me something even more precious: my mother's freedom.

I shake my head, virtually at a loss for words. "Thank you, Nick. This is a gift I can never repay."

"I'll never ask you to. Besides, money has its advantages. Why not make full use of them?"

"Is that how you justified what you did to me?" The question blurts off my tongue before I can stop it. I want to be grateful for the risks and the expense he's no doubt taken to help my mom, but the wounded part of me is still bitter and confused about the way Nick manipulated my life when we first met. Now that I've said it, there's little point in talking about anything else until we get past it.

If we can get past it.

He slows beside me on the sidewalk. I pause, too, feeling as if we've reached the end of our path here today. His face is so hard to read, sober and contemplative, yet filled with a torment that takes me aback.

"I owe you an apology, Avery. For everything."

I shake my head. "No, Nick. You owe me answers. I don't need an apology unless you can make me understand how you could do what you did. I need you to make me understand why."

People jostle past us on both sides, more than one turning an askance look on us as my voice rises with the hurt and confusion I've been holding inside for the better part of a year. I don't care if I'm creating a bit of a scene right here in the middle of Fifth Avenue. All of the emotion that's been trapped inside me percolates to the surface as if the wounds are still fresh.

In so many ways, they are.

So is the depth of what I still feel for this man.

"Dammit, Nick, I need to know what the hell I meant to you—if I meant a damn thing at all."

He doesn't say anything for what seems like an eternity. His handsome face is grim, uncertain. It's only in that moment that I realize where we are. Where we've stopped.

I glance at the large window behind him, then up at the sign above the door.

"Dominion," I murmur.

Nick's gallery. The one where some of my art used to hang before he and I ever met. Before we knew anything about each other. Or so I believed.

"You brought me here deliberately?"

"If you want answers, Avery, then we need to start at the beginning."

8

I wait, confused and apprehensive, as Nick unlocks the gallery door and gestures for me to step inside with him. Dominion is closed today. The invitingly contemporary space is dim and unlit except for the sunlight coming in from the street, the only sounds the continuous drone of rushing traffic punctuated by the occasional blast of vehicle horn or wail of a siren.

I've been to Nick's gallery more than a few times, yet as I cross the threshold with him now I feel as though I'm stepping into foreign territory. I can't imagine what he means by bringing me here, and something inside me is afraid to guess. The grave look he gives me as we enter does nothing to reassure me.

"What's going on, Nick?"

He doesn't answer. The anxiety I felt at the door

deepens into dread as he leads me soberly through the main exhibit room of the gallery, past the dozens of remarkable paintings displayed on the walls. My gaze catches on one particular piece—a haunting, startlingly intimate work titled *Beauty*. It seems like forever since I've seen this portrait of Kathryn Tremont. Not since the beginning of my time with Nick.

A memory of that night flashes through my mind. He and I standing in front of *Beauty,* speaking to each other for the first time. That piercing cerulean gaze enthralling me, seeing through to the most naked corners of my soul while in a single conversation he wickedly, expertly, peeled away my secrets, my desires, and my self-control.

We left the gallery together that night and headed straight to his bed.

Reckless. That's what I called it then, what I know it to be with even more certainty after all this time and heartache later.

But that night isn't the beginning Nick is taking me back to. I realize this as he continues farther into the gallery, toward a darkened hallway away from the main exhibition area.

I can sense there is something more that I don't know, something bigger. Something I may not want to see any more than he seems eager to show me.

At the end of the hall we reach a closed door with a small metal sign marked PRIVATE.

Nick stops here and glances at me. "I haven't been in here in almost two years. No one has."

For the first time, I see doubt in his eyes.

I see shame.

I don't know what lurks behind the door to this

room, but based on his bleak expression I'm already dreading what I'll find. "Nick, please. You're scaring me. Tell me what this is about."

"The truth."

There is a keypad panel on the wall. He taps a five-digit code and I hear a soft snick as the lock disengages. I don't move, can hardly draw air into my lungs as he opens the door then walks inside the pitch-dark room.

I take a hesitant step behind him just as he flicks on the lights.

Bright fluorescents burst to life overhead. My vision goes white momentarily, shocked by the sudden explosion of light in the darkness.

And then another kind of shock settles over me.

The room is a small private office. At least it appears it had been at one time. A cherry-wood desk lies broken, upturned in the center of the room. The chair that likely used to sit behind it has been savaged, too, little more than a splintered heap of tinder amid a sea of scattered paper, books, and smashed objets d'art.

Paint covers everything. Everywhere I look, violent splashes of red and black and a dozen other dark colors have congealed and dried wherever they were thrown. There is so much rage in this room, so much wreckage, I can't hold back my gasp as I take it all in.

And then I see it.

The easel tilted drunkenly in the far corner of all this savagery.

A canvas barely clings to its perch on the wooden stand. It, too, has been brutalized.

Beneath the furious brush marks that strive to conceal it is a painting rendered in crude, halting movement. There is no finesse in the half-completed work, only frustration. It's been abandoned. Aborted.

Ruthlessly destroyed.

Just like the rest of this room.

At my side, Nick watches me absorb the totality of the destruction before me.

"You did this." I look at him in question, struggling to reconcile the strong, powerful man next to me and the utter lack of control manifested in this space.

I can't fathom the despair, the hopelessness.

He moves away from me, deeper into the awful time capsule of violence and ruin. "I don't recall what made me decide to come here that night," he says, his voice toneless, his spine rigid. "It was late. I was drunk."

As he speaks, I notice the empty liquor bottle nestled among the debris. Not the high-brow single malt whisky I've seen him drink from time to time, but a cheap fifth of rotgut that likely didn't cost him more than twenty dollars.

He pivots, raking his palm over the top of his dark hair as he surveys the room. "Evidently, I decided it was a good night to paint. You can see how well that went."

He chuckles humorlessly and holds up his scarred right hand, the one he nearly lost many years ago during an argument with his father. That careless altercation when Nick was eighteen—and whatever spurred it—isn't something he has shared with me in any great detail. All I know is that in the end his father slammed him through a plate glass window.

Nick could have died. He was fortunate in that, but his injuries were horrific enough. Much of his arm and most of the tendons in his hand were shredded. The hand Nick used to paint with ruined in one irreparable moment.

His artistic gift lost before it had the chance to soar.

I've never seen his art, but Kathryn Tremont has. To hear her describe it, Nick's talent was extraordinary, among the best she had ever seen. His rage over losing that part of him was deep and volatile. Until now, given all of his success in business and the fortune he's amassed because of it, I believed Nick had come to terms with the loss of his art.

This room says otherwise.

It screams Nick's pain with an agony that staggers me.

"I had a gun with me that night," he says, no emotion in his deep voice. All I see in his eyes is raw, terrifying truth. "I was tired and angry and . . . Christ, so fucking empty. I remember thinking that night that I just wanted it to stop. I needed it all to end."

A knot of ice-cold fear lodges in my throat as I listen to his confession. Dominic Baine, who to the rest of the world has everything he could possibly want or need, is telling me that the last time he stepped foot in this room he could think of no good reason to live.

I swallow past my dread, barely resisting the urge to offer him comfort. He won't accept it. I can see that in the stoic way he stands, well out of my reach. If I try to close the distance between us right now it will only push him further away.

And he's not finished telling me everything he needs to say.

"I passed out in the gallery at some point. I don't remember leaving the room, but when I eventually came to, I still had the gun in my hand. I opened my eyes and the first thing I saw was a black-and-white portrait hanging on the wall out there." He slowly swivels his head in my direction. "Your painting."

I nod faintly, because I know this part of the story. The first painting I ever completed had been on display at Dominion months before I met Dominic Baine. More recently, on our way to Paris last year, I discovered that same painting hanging in in Nick's state room aboard his private jet.

"I didn't realize I was looking at a self-portrait at the time." His gaze holds me with such open admiration it steals my breath. "All I saw was an arresting beauty—and a hauntedness—that refused to release me. I couldn't look away from it. Couldn't look away from you, Avery."

As unsettling as it had been to realize in Paris that it was some degree of obsession that brought Nick into my life, right now the primary emotion I feel is relief. Relief that he is standing here in front of me at all. Relief that he found some reason to hang on that night, even if the price was my own heart.

"I took your painting home with me. For the next three days, all I could think about was the face on that canvas and that fucking forty-five in my hand. I knew that sooner or later, it was going to come down to just one of them." He walks toward me, his movements slow, but far from uncertain. "I can't tell you all the things I felt when I looked at your image in the painting. Fascination. Adoration. A powerful, irresistible desire for a woman I thought was too incredible to be real. Things I feel every time I look at you."

He reaches out and I hold my breath as his fingers brush gently along my cheek. I didn't come here to be seduced, maybe not even to forgive, but intentions and boundaries have always been blurred when it comes to

Nick and me. The soft sigh that slips past my lips only confirms that truth.

"I wanted the woman in the painting more than anything, Avery. Even death." His touch leaves me, his hand drifting down to his side. "As for the talent I saw in that particular piece, it amazed me. Your gift was so raw, yet unmistakable. I looked at your art in that one painting and I felt awe and respect. Jealousy. Even rage. What I didn't feel was empty. I threw the gun away, and that next day I went back to the gallery to find out everything I could about the painting. When Margot told me the artist and the model were one and the same, I had to know more. I had to know you."

"Nick . . . I'm not sure how to respond to all of this. I'm not sure what to think."

It's going to take some time to process everything he's saying and how I feel about it. Inside I'm breaking at the knowledge of how dark his life had gotten before we met. I'm humbled to think that I had anything to do with bringing him back from that brink.

My life had been dark before Nick too. My past had a grip on me I hadn't been able to break on my own. In so many ways, he saved me every bit as much as I saved him. It was our mutual secrets that destroyed us. If we stand any chance of moving past them, we have to drag them all into the light.

I shake my head, trying to cling to the reason we're both here. "You lied to me. From the very beginning and for all those months afterward, you let me think our meeting was purely coincidence when you orchestrated every facet of our relationship. You made certain that every path I took would lead me straight to you. For God's sake, you even bought the apartment building I was living in and turned it into expensive condos to ensure I couldn't stay there."

"Yes, I did." His expression is sober, but hardly contrite. "I learned that you were living in a dump at the mercy of a slum lord. It was unacceptable, so I gave you a reason to leave. And then I gave you someplace better to go."

I tilt a wry look at him. "You hired Claire Prentice to come into Vendange where I was working and pretend she needed a house sitter. In your high-priced Park Avenue building where you also happened to live."

"I wanted to know you were somewhere safe and comfortable. I wanted to remove the obstacles that stood in the way of you and the potential of your art. I wanted to see your talent set free to become what it has now. Most of all, I wanted you close to me, so I could get to know you."

"You're serious."

"You wanted the truth," he says softly. "Now, you have it."

I had convinced myself that he had played me for a fool, that all of his manipulations and the efforts he took to conceal them from me had been some kind of sick game. I thought he used me simply for his own amusement, but it's hard to reconcile any of that now. It's impossible to ignore the earnestness in his eyes. As twisted as his actions were, there's no denying that they came from a place of genuine concern.

"How can you make something so fucked up sound so well-meaning, as if what you did is the most reasonable thing in the world?" I heave a conflicted sigh. "Why not just ask me out like a normal person?"

He gives me a smile that's full of irony. "I never said

I was normal. You know that better than anyone."

"I can't make jokes about this, Nick. Jesus, not after everything you just told me. Not after everything you put me through."

"I know, and I'm sorry about that. All of it." His gaze searches mine, tender but unflinching. "I told you in the beginning that I wasn't prepared for how much I craved you, how much you meant to me. I wanted the woman I saw in your painting. I wanted to help shape the talent I saw in your art, the talent I no longer had. But I wasn't prepared for you, Avery. I sure as hell wasn't planning on falling in love with you."

I close my eyes against the yearning those words open inside me. Now, at this distance, with this new clarity, I recall the things he said while we were together. All of the clues he gave me along the way. The warnings that he wasn't a good man, that he never wanted to hurt me.

He'd been telling me all along, but I was too swept up in him—in the fantasy of who I became with him—to hear it.

"I know nothing will excuse what I did, Avery. My reasons don't justify anything. No apology can make this right between us. But I am sorry for hurting you, for deceiving you." He strokes my face with a caress that's so gentle it wrings a small moan from deep inside me. "I will always be sorry for the hurt I've caused you. And no matter where we go from here, I will always love you."

"No." It takes every bit of my will to withdraw from his touch. My head is spinning in confusion, my heart swamped by too many emotions for me to sort out, especially when he's touching me, looking at me with such raw honesty I can barely breathe.

"What do you want from me, Nick? What are you trying to do? It's been a year since we've even seen each other, and don't tell me that wasn't deliberate. You severed all connections to me after Paris, including the sale of Vendange. If not for the other night at the university, we wouldn't even be having this conversation."

"You're right." He nods solemnly. "I wanted to give you space, freedom. I didn't see any other way than to remove myself from your life completely. If I hadn't, I knew it would only drive you further away."

I can't argue with his reasoning. There were countless times I thought of running away from New York. It would have been easier than staying in the place that held so many memories of the two of us. But I was trying to build a life here. I had built one for myself, even if it no longer included Nick.

Even if my heart broke a little bit more every day I spent apart from him.

"Why did you wait so long to tell me all of this? You could've come after me in Paris. You could've made me listen, but you didn't. You didn't even try."

"I did try, Avery." His dark brows furrow over his sober stare. "I did come after you. I made it all the way to the airport. I tried to force my way through security to try to catch you before you left." He exhales a short breath. "I threw a swing at one of the soldiers who blocked my way at the gate. He landed his fist in my face, then he and three other armed guards took me down. I spent the night in a Paris hospital with a fractured jaw."

I listen, torn between astonishment that he actually did follow me to the airport and concern for what he risked in trying to reach me. "The soldiers you struck might have sent you to jail instead of the hospital, Nick. God, they might've killed you."

He shrugs it off with little more than a bland look. "I came after you, Avery. I wasn't going to let you leave without hearing me out. But later, lying in the hospital after you were back home in the States, I knew it was better for you that you'd gone. Paris was supposed to be a fresh start for us. I thought it still could be for you, but that meant setting you free. I held myself to that promise this past year. And then I saw you at that reception the other night."

My heart pounds in my breast as he moves closer to me. He knows I won't stop him now. He knows I need him every bit as much as he needs me. With nothing but a breath to separate us, he brings his hand up, settling it warmly, intimately around my nape.

I'm not certain if he draws me to him or if I drift there out of instinct and yearning. It hardly matters, because in that next moment, his mouth lowers to mine. I moan as he kisses me, unable to deny the visceral expression of my longing . . . and my relief.

His touch feels too good on my skin, his lips on mine so achingly familiar and welcome.

God, what am I doing?

He's already broken my heart once.

He's wrecked me.

Yet here I am, ready for ruin all over again.

I moan again, but this time it's a pained sound. My hands come up between us, pressing flat against the firm planes of his chest.

"I can't do this." I back away from him, my lips still tingling and wet from his kiss. I want more of him. I want it with a ferocity that terrifies me. "Nick, I'm not ready for this again. I—I have to go."

I pivot and take a step toward the open door. Nick's fingers shackle loosely around my wrist. "Don't run, Avery. Please." His voice is rough with arousal and something I hardly recognize in him. Fear. Vulnerability. "Please, don't run away from me again."

He doesn't resist when I withdraw from his grasp, but his darkened blue eyes implore me to stay. "I just can't, Nick. I'm not running, but I do need time. I need to think about all of this . . . about what all of this means. I can't do that when you're touching me, when you're kissing me."

"Then I'll stop."

I exhale a soft laugh. "You and I both know where this will go if I stay any longer."

"Are you saying you can't resist me?"

A ghost of a smile plays at the edge of his sinful mouth, the first real spark of humor—of light—I've seen in him since we arrived here. It's tempting to give in to it, to give in to him. But I have to be cautious this time. I have to protect my heart.

My foolish, reckless heart that urges me to turn back into Nick's arms and to hell with the consequences.

But my head is stronger now.

If barely.

"I have to go, Nick."

He holds my gaze as he lets his hands fall slowly to his sides. "Will you come back?"

Come back to him, he means. The truth is, I don't know if I'm ready for that.

I'm not sure I ever will be.

I think about the pain he caused me. The anguish that came from loving him, from believing I could trust him, that he had no reason to hide anything from me. I thought I was the only one with damning secrets that could destroy us.

But I can't think about the pain Nick caused me without acknowledging the pleasure too. The passion that's still pulsing between us now, just waiting to ignite.

Will the risk of getting hurt again be worth the promise of everything else we could have? I'm not certain. I can't know anything for sure so long as Nick is looking at me like I'm the only woman in the world. The only woman he wants, needs . . . loves.

I move farther away from him, desperate for the physical distance.

"I'm not running away from you, Nick. But I don't know if I can come back. Not like we were before."

He nods gravely, something in his eyes shuttering now. I search for the right words, but I'm too raw to articulate everything I'm feeling. And overriding it all is confusion. Fear. A need for solid ground.

"Try to understand," I murmur lamely. "I just . . . I have to go."

I feel the heat of him behind me as I step out to the gallery hallway, but he doesn't stop me.

Thankfully, he stays inside as I walk calmly out the door. He won't see that I break into a hurried jog as soon as I'm out of his view.

He won't know there are hot tears clogging my throat and stinging my eyes as the cacophony of the city swallows me up.

9

Three nights later, I'm still trying to decide how I feel about everything Nick said. I'm still trying to convince myself that I did the best thing—the only sane thing—in telling him I needed time apart in order to think, to process.

I may never fully understand what he did. I know I'll never be able to fathom why it was my painting—my face—that captivated him so completely. Will it ever make sense to me that Dominic Baine, a man who can have anything and anyone he desires somehow chose to love me?

No, I'm sure I'll never begin to understand that.

As for the rest, I only wish I could pretend that I don't know anything about the dark place Nick had been that night, drunk and alone in his private office at the back of the gallery. But I do know about that. I know what it's like to feel broken. To feel irreparably damaged. Angry and hopeless. Empty.

I know because I've been there too.

If Nick had never entered my life, I might still be there.

If not for him, I might still be lost, still running away from the past that nearly destroyed me. Still afraid to believe my life would ever get better, that I might ever be happy.

Or worthy of being loved.

Regardless of his motives, Nick has given me more than any man I've ever known. I love him with every fiber of my being, yet I'm allowing fear and insecurity drive a deeper wedge between us.

I thought time away from him would be easier for me. I should have known, it's never easy being separated from Nick. A year's worth of practice wasn't enough the first time. Now that I know he still cares for me—after hearing him say that he's still in love with me—the only place I truly want to be is back in his arms.

"God, I'm an idiot."

Standing beside me in a glittering hotel ballroom full of Manhattan's gowned and tuxedoed elite, my friend Lita lifts her brows as she stares at me over the rim of her champagne glass. "An idiot for bringing me as your date to this fancy shindig? Don't say I didn't warn you. These aren't exactly my people."

It's true, she was reluctant to come with me. Complaining she had nothing suitable to wear to Kathryn Tremont's foundation auction at the elegant five-star hotel, Lita is absolutely beautiful in a vintage-looking black tea-length dress with chiffon sleeves that veil her tattooed arms in mystery and sweet kitten heels. The outfit, she informed me when we met outside the hotel tonight, is actually a theater costume she got on loan from a designer friend who works off-Broadway.

"You're not the problem," I tell her. "And you look amazing, by the way. Thank you again for stepping in tonight on short notice. I really didn't want to come alone."

She eyes me narrowly as I take a sip from my glass. "Then what's the matter? You having second thoughts about breaking up with Brandon?"

"No, it's not that. Ending things with Brandon is the only smart decision I've made in the past several days."

"Smart and overdue," she says. "He seems like a nice guy and all, but the two of you didn't make a lot of sense if you ask me."

I concede with a small nod. "You're right about him on both counts. He was totally accepting when I told him I didn't want to see him anymore. And since he didn't seem surprised or upset, it only confirmed that I was making the right choice for both of us."

Lita tilts her glass toward mine. "Here's to making smart choices."

We both take a drink, but she's still looking at me expectantly. "What?"

"I'm almost afraid to ask where the idiocy part comes in." Her ruby-red stained lips purse for an instant. "Oh, shit. Tell me this is not about Dominic-fucking-Baine."

At that same moment, some of Kathryn's society friends glide past Lita and me on their way to circulate with other guests. The pack of glamorous older women pause to say hello to me, temporarily stalling the lecture

I'm certain is coming from my friend.

Lita smiles and politely shakes hands as I introduce her, but she doesn't miss a beat once we're alone again. "Have you hopped back into bed with that asshole? Because then we're talking about idiot choices."

"Nick's not an asshole." I blow out a resigned sigh. "Well, sometimes he is. But that's beside the point. And no, I haven't slept with him."

"But you want to and that's almost as bad." She hands her empty glass to a passing waiter then folds her arms, studying me as if I've lost my mind. "You still love him, don't you?"

I shrug and down the last swallow of my champagne.

"What happened to 'I'm over him, I've moved on, end of story?'"

"I'm not, I haven't, and . . . maybe it isn't."

"Idiot." Lita rolls her eyes, but she's also laughing. "And now you just cost me fifty bucks to Matt."

My mouth drops open. "You two had money riding on whether I'd get back together with Nick?"

She holds up her hands in mock surrender. "Hey, the money was Matt's idea. I wanted him to clean the studio for a month if I won."

I snort in spite of myself. "Jerks."

Lita grins. "Yeah, but what would you do without us?"

We're still laughing when I feel a strong, warm palm settle against the center of my back. A masculine hand, no doubt about it. Given Nick's tangled, acrimonious past with Kathryn Tremont, I don't expect to see him anywhere near this event, but that doesn't keep my heart from leaping in surprise—in tempered hope—as I turn my head to see who's behind me.

The tall, broad-shouldered man with the long, wavy brown hair and the slow, sexy grin that's now trained on me isn't Nick, but I'm still happy to see him.

"Jared! Hi."

"Avery." He leans down and kisses my cheek. "Always a pleasure to see you, darlin'," he says in his smooth southern drawl. Framed in thick lashes, his molasses-brown eyes drink me in without a trace of shame. "Kathryn mentioned you were coming tonight. Unfortunately, she also mentioned that you were seeing someone. Which of these tuxedoed monkeys is the lucky guy?"

I can't help but smile at Jared's laid-back bad-boy charm. Looking at him it would be easy to mistake the muscular, ruggedly handsome man for a blue jeans model or a displaced cowboy out for a good time in the big city, but Jared Rush's talent far exceeds his panty-melting looks.

A renowned painter whose edgy portraits fetch millions, Jared is also a close friend of Kathryn Tremont's. In fact, she posed for him years ago when he painted *Beauty*, the unflinchingly intimate portrait of her on display at Dominion.

"I guess I'm the lucky guy," Lita blurts. "I mean, not that I'm a guy. And not that Avery and I are dating or anything. We're only together for tonight. But not together-together. Shit." She winces, her teeth sinking into her lip as if to stanch the uncontrolled flow of words from pouring out of her mouth. Awkwardly, she clears her throat. "We're friends."

Jared chuckles. I stare at Lita wide-eyed and amused. It's rare to see my tough friend rattled. And while Jared has that effect on most women, I suspect Lita's awe is more professional in nature.

Still smiling, I make the introductions. "Jared Rush, this is my good friend and fellow artist Lita Frasier. We share studio space in East Harlem."

He extends his hand to her. "Lita, honored to meet you. Aren't you the artist commissioned to do the lobby sculpture for the Dektech building over in Brooklyn Heights?"

Her jaw goes slack. "I . . . um, yeah. I am. That is, I was. I, uh, sort of quit today."

I gape at her. "You what?" I know how excited she was to land the high-profile job, how immersed she's been in the original work of art she designed for Derek Kingston's new office building. "Lita, what happened?"

"Suffice it to say the project parameters changed midstream and I can't work like that." She gives me a look that speaks volumes. It also warns me that she doesn't want to discuss it in front of Jared.

"Sorry to hear it," he says, then quirks a cocky smile. "I don't know Kingston personally, but I've heard he can be a tyrant to work with."

"When he's not being an absolute toddler," Lita mutters.

Jared laughs. "Remember, we're talking about a man who's gone from world-famous rockstar to billionaire tech CEO practically overnight. I suppose toddler and tyrant are two sides of that same coin."

Lita huffs. "Yeah, well, Derek will have to try to cash that coin in with someone else. I'm out."

"His loss, I'm sure," Jared says. He glances my way, turning the full impact of that megawatt smile on me now. "Will you be around after the auction? I have to go play emcee for Kathryn now, but I'd love the chance to catch up. I'll come find you."

He doesn't wait for me to answer. With typical Jared charm and swagger, he tells Lita it was a pleasure to meet her, then heads off for the stage, the clusters of auction attendees cutting a path for him as he strolls through the center of the gathered crowd.

"Wow," Lita murmurs after he's gone. "So, that's Jared Rush."

"That's him." I glance at her, frowning. "You want to tell me what happened between you and Derek Kingston today?"

"Not really." She gives me an exasperated look. "You know I will. But first, the ladies' room, okay? It's gonna take me ten minutes just to figure out how to pee in this dress."

We exit the ballroom and instead of turning left outside the doors where dozens of other women are headed, I take Lita in the other direction, toward a quiet hallway off the beaten path.

"Are you sure we're going the right way?" she asks as we turn a corner and the din of the party grows fainter behind us.

"One benefit of attending these kinds of events with Nick is that I also learned where to find the best restroom options." I wink at her as I push open the creamy door to the ladies' room and we step inside to blessed peace and quiet spread out before us in soothing cream and gold tones. Best of all, no lines.

Lita grins. "You're a genius. Now help me unzip this fucking dress before I burs—"

A low moan interrupts us.

It's a faint, but anguished sound, coming from the farthest stall.

"Hello?" I call out. Lita tries to hold me back, but I shake my head and walk cautiously toward the sound as it comes again, more pained this time. On the heels of it, a thready wheeze.

The stall door is closed, no gap beneath it and the louvered shutters that make up the panel are there for privacy, showing nothing of the occupant who's clearly in serious distress.

"Hello?" I say again. "Are you all right in there?"

A small, shaky voice answers me. "Avery?"

"Oh, my God." I glance back at Lita in alarm. "It's Kathryn."

I grab for the latch on the stall door, but it's locked from inside.

"Kathryn, what happened? Do you need your medicine?"

Lita is right beside me now, her expression looking about as anxious and helpless as I feel. I jiggle the latch again, but the damn thing doesn't give.

"Freaking high-class bathrooms and their sturdy doors," Lita grumbles under breath. "Do you want me to try to kick it in?"

She's already taking off her kitten heels. I shake my head, frowning. Inside the stall, Kathryn groans again, weaker than before. Then she retches violently.

"Shit, Avery. Don't you think we should call someone to help—"

"No." This time it's Kathryn who answers. Her raspy shout is full of agony, but it's also sharp with authority. "Goddamn it, don't call anyone."

Behind the closed door she's panting, still wheezing with the misery of her advancing disease. The toilet flushes. After a moment, I hear the rustle of a long silk skirt, the unsteady scrape of a high heel on the polished marble floor.

The lock snicks free, then Kathryn Tremont slowly opens the stall door. I haven't seen her for a couple of weeks, yet the woman I'm looking at now seems to have aged ten years since then. Her late-stage cancer is to blame for that. Kathryn's lovely face is gaunt and ashen. Her steel-gray hair, still elegant in its twisted chignon, is dull beneath the soft light of the ladies' room. Her wise, dark eyes hold me in an affectionate, if pleading, stare.

"I'm fine now," she murmurs behind the wadded length of toilet tissue she holds to her mouth. "I just need a little drink of water . . . and some . . . air."

She takes half a step out of the stall before her knees give out and her tall, frail body begins to sag toward the floor. Lita and I both leap into action, each of us taking an arm and carefully helping Kathryn out to one of the cushioned settees in the adjacent washroom.

I'm taken aback by the extent of her weakness. With her eyes closed and her rail-thin body slumped into the small sofa, it's a stark reminder of just how far Kathryn's cancer has advanced. Lita recognizes it too.

"I'll get some water," she says, leaving me to try to reason with our unexpected charge.

I press the back of my hand to Kathryn's brow. Her skin is clammy, but her forehead is burning up. "How do you feel?" I ask quietly.

Her cracked, pale lips stretch into a wry smile. "Like I'm dying, dear."

She attempts to sit up, but can barely manage to lift her shoulders off the cushioned seat. "You need rest, Kathryn. I know you don't want to hear it, but I think you need to go to the hospital."

"For what? So they can run a bunch of tests and tell me I'm dying?" She barks out a rattling laugh. "I'm a tough old bird. I'm going to go when I'm damn good and ready."

I smile sadly, shaking my head. "I think your stubbornness is what's gotten you this far."

"Don't you forget it." Her eyelids lift and I see a small spark of determination light in her weary gaze. "Help me up now. I need to get back to the ballroom."

I'm skeptical, but I say nothing as Lita brings a disposable cup of water from the tap and hunkers down in front of Kathryn to give it to her. Kathryn's hands shake terribly, but she succeeds in taking a few small sips.

"All right, let's get on with it," she says, pushing the cup back at Lita. "I feel much better now."

Lita's glance is as dubious as mine, but we do our best to assist Kathryn to her feet. Her limbs feel boneless, uncooperative beneath her. After a couple of failed attempts to stand, she sinks back down onto the settee with a deep sigh.

"You need to be in bed resting," I tell her. "If you won't go to a hospital then you need to let me find someone to take you home. Where's your driver tonight?"

"I can't leave now," she mumbles, already fading again. "Tell my driver I have to . . . I have to get to the hotel before . . . the auction starts . . ."

"Go find Jared," I instruct Lita as Kathryn slips into a faint. "Explain the situation to him and let him know I'm going to make sure she gets home. He's going to have to carry the whole event tonight and make some kind of excuse to cover Kathryn's absence. He'll know what to do."

Lita nods. "You're sure we shouldn't call 911 or something?"

"There's nothing any of those people can do for her." I exhale an ironic, humorless breath. "Kathryn Tremont would rather die than create a scene with an ambulance and a stretcher carrying her out of her own soiree." I glance back down at the woman who's become an unlikely friend and confidante to me. "I'll make sure she's taken care of."

Lita casts me a sober look. "Keep me posted. Call me if you need anything."

I nod. "Thanks, Lita."

After she goes, I retrieve Kathryn's evening bag from where she dropped it in the bathroom stall. Her cell phone is locked with a passcode, so there's no way for me to call her driver even if I could find the number in her contacts.

"Shit." I'm not about to leave her alone to go looking for him. I walk back out to where she's slumped on the sofa, her breathing shallow, her fever still burning under my fingertips as I gently stroke her brow.

I deliberate only for a moment before I reach into my small clutch and push the number I still know by heart.

"Nick?" I murmur as soon as I hear his deep voice answer. "I need you. Please, come now."

10

Bring her around this way, Nick." Avery glances back at me as I carry Kathryn from my car toward the palatial Fifth Avenue residence.

I had been waiting nearly four days for some word from her, trying my damnedest to uphold my agreement to give Avery time and space to decide if there was still anything left between us to salvage. I would have gone to her anytime, under any condition she set, but nothing could have kept me from her once I heard her emotion-choked voice on the other end of the line.

Not even my acrimonious past with the unresponsive woman draped lifelessly in my arms.

I may have my reasons for mistrust when it comes to Kathryn Tremont, but it's obvious that she means something to Avery. What's also painfully obvious is the fact that Kathryn's health is even worse than I realized. She's little more than a bag of bones in my arms, the vibrant force of nature I met when I first arrived in New York eaten away by the cancer she's been fighting off and on for nearly a decade.

At the mansion's back door Avery and I are met by a couple of household staff, one of them an olive-skinned male who looks attractive enough to be a runway model and young enough to be Kathryn's grandson. The other attendant is a sturdy middle-aged female wearing crisp nurse's whites, her graying ginger hair scraped into an austere bun on top of her head.

The male's eyes go wide with alarm as soon as they light on us, a small, helpless noise leaking out of him. The nurse looks equally concerned, but wastes no time getting to work.

"Stubborn woman. I tried to tell her she was in no shape to be going out tonight." Pushing aside Kathryn's apparent flavor-of-the-month, the nurse motions for Avery and me to follow her. "All right, let's get her in bed and comfortable so I can stabilize her and check her vitals."

Avery walks soberly alongside me as we follow the attendant through the sprawling residence. Instead of going upstairs to one of the ten bedrooms I know are located on the second floor, we are led past a pair of tall double doors that open into the opulent salon at the front of the house.

The art-filled chamber where Kathryn used to entertain the most elite of Manhattan's social scene has been transformed into a private hospital suite. The fortune in paintings and sculpture still remains inside the high-ceilinged room, but the new focal point is a king-size adjustable bed draped in a champagne silk duvet and flanked by wheeled medical machines and portable IV stands. A table cluttered with enough prescription bottles and pain killers to outfit a small pharmacy sits off to the side of the bed.

Christ. I knew Kathryn's condition was grave, but I wasn't prepared for this. I keep my shock contained as I place her on the mattress. At least, I think I do. Avery senses my reaction as soon as our eyes meet.

"Kathryn's been living down here for more than six months now. The stairs have been out of the question for a long time, and the elevator only makes her nausea worse." As I move away from the bed to let the nurse take over, Avery gives me a sad smile. "She's going to be livid when she finds out she had to be carried into her house like an invalid tonight."

I grunt, knowing it's true. "Especially by me."

"Probably," she admits, lifting her shoulder in a vague shrug. "Thank you for being here, Nick. I didn't mean to pull you away from your other business tonight. Another late night with a client?"

She's looking at my dark suit and white dress shirt, which is unbuttoned at my throat. Although she doesn't say it, I have to wonder if she's picturing me having dinner with another female like Simone Emmons from last week. If she suspects I'm being anything but honest with her, it's too hard to tell for all the weariness I see in her face.

"I was on a video conference with my team in Melbourne when you called. We're in the middle of acquiring a large residential tower over there and some of the Australian regulations are slowing the whole thing to a standstill. I left Beck in charge of the meeting and drove straight over to get you."

"I'm sorry," she murmurs. "I didn't know who else to call."

"There's nothing to be sorry about. Business can wait. I don't want you to call anyone else." I give in to the urge to sweep aside a tendril of golden hair that curls against her cheek. "I'm here for you, Avery. That's never going to change."

The fact that she doesn't withdraw sends a warm current of hope through me. I'm not going to bullshit myself into thinking she reached out to me due to anything more than necessity or desperation tonight, but it's a start.

Avery glances toward the bed, where Kathryn's nurse has begun to attend her. "I ought to see if there's anything I can do to help."

I should offer to do the same, but being in a room so full of sickness and painful, prolonged dying is almost too much for me to take.

Before a lot of old rusty memories have the chance to churn to life in my head and make me feel like any more of a pussy, I nod at Avery. "It's all right. Take all the time you need. I'll be here if you need me."

"You don't have to wait around, Nick. It could be a while before I'm comfortable leaving her."

"Avery, I'll be here."

She stares at me for a long moment, then turns away and quietly goes to Kathryn's bedside.

I don't linger in the room. The cloying scent of antiseptic is already drilling into my skull, though not sharp enough to mask the odor of disease. All of it makes my throat close up and a cold sweat break out on the back of my neck.

I step out to the hallway and breathe in the cool, fresher air.

It's been roughly thirteen years since I've been inside this house. I was a kid, barely twenty when Kathryn Tremont brought me here for the first time. Our relationship was brief and mutually advantageous. She was looking for someone new to decorate her arm at social events and make her feel alive in bed. I was looking for myself. I was trying to figure out who I might be able to become in a city that was about as far away from my father's home in the Florida Keys as I could get with nothing but one good hand to work with and a hundred bucks in my pocket.

It was Kathryn who introduced me to this glittering world I also inhabit now.

She gave me a taste for fine things. She introduced me to people who taught me about money and business—albeit, not as their peer, but as the disregarded boy-toy who quickly learned the value of listening and observation. I absorbed every conversation I heard. I learned everything I could from the rich, arrogant fucks who talked as openly around me at cocktail parties as they did any other unimportant service attendant.

I wanted to be one of those rich, arrogant fucks too. I wanted to be as different as I possibly could be from the poor, powerless kid I was when I left Florida.

I wanted to belong in this immense, indomitable city. I wanted to own it.

And I was so damn sure I could—until the day Kathryn unwittingly invited my past back to haunt me. To be fair, I know she didn't realize how deeply I hated my art, especially then. It was a reminder of where I'd come from, what I'd lived through. A reminder of everything I'd lost simply because of the fucked up world into which I'd been born.

Kathryn knew of my hatred for my father. She knew about the drunken fight I had with him and the resulting injuries that cost me all but the most basic use of my hand.

Thanks to Avery's friendship with Kathryn, she knows all of this too.

Fortunately, neither of them know the reason why.

That's a shame I intend to take with me to my grave. Hell, I'd hasten the journey before I'd let Avery get anywhere close to the pitiful reality of my past.

Thinking about that part of my life makes me restless. My muscles twitch with the need to be moving, to be doing something—anything—rather than standing around revisiting old ghosts I left for dead a long time ago.

I stroll back the way we came in, recalling there is a terrace patio off the formal dining room on the other side of the sprawling residence. Outside the French doors, the summer night air is cool and refreshing. I fill my lungs with it, trying to purge the medicinal stench that still clings to the back of my throat.

I'm not the only one who fled the house. Kathryn's young male companion is out here too. He nods at me in greeting from where he is reclined on a sun chair in the dark, the burning end of his cigarette glowing bright orange as he takes a long drag.

"Those will kill you, you know."

A flash of perfect white teeth as he smiles. "Sooner or later, something will, right? I'm Michael."

"Nick," I say, closing the glass-paned door and leaning my shoulder against it. "Have you known her for long?"

He shakes his head. "Couple of months. You?"

I don't answer. What would be the point? This kid doesn't know Kathryn Tremont, and in another couple of months he'll be rotated out for a new distraction. If she lasts that long. I doubt very much that she will.

Which means Avery is going to be hurting all over again when that happens. Her friendship with Kathryn is a fact I can't ignore any more than I can control it.

One thing I've learned about Avery is that I can't stop her from caring about someone. Her heart is too big, too pure.

How else could she ever have loved me?

I stand outside for a good while, long after Michael has finished his smoke and sauntered off into the darkness to take a phone call in private. When I head back into the house, Avery meets me in the hallway. She's just come out of Kathryn's makeshift bedroom, her lovely face tired and drawn.

"How's she doing?"

"She woke up for a couple of minutes, but she's sleeping now. Evidently she's been pushing herself too hard planning the auction fundraiser, trying to do too much when she really needs to slow down."

I nod in agreement, even though I doubt Kathryn will ever subscribe to that plan. She used to joke that she'd have time to sleep when she was dead. After seeing her condition tonight, I can't find much humor in the idea.

"Her fever's still pretty high," Avery adds. "She's in a lot of pain, more than she's been letting on. Her nurse just gave her some morphine to take the edge off and help her relax for the night."

"I'm sorry." It's all I can think of to say. I don't do well in these situations under normal circumstances, whatever that is. Seeing Avery struggle to cope only makes me feel even less equipped to deal with Kathryn's illness. "Is there anything I can do for you?"

She looks at me with weary, sorrow-filled eyes. "Will you take me home now?"

"Of course, I can do that." I reach out, cupping my palm against her cheek. "Let's go."

We no sooner get on the road than Avery's phone rings with an incoming call. I tense, dreading it's Kathryn's nurse with worsening news. The reality is only slightly better.

"Jared, hi. I'm sorry I forgot to call you."

Jared Rush's voice is a low, indistinct rumble on the other end of the line. I don't like the jealousy that flares in me. The suspicion that one of my old friends apparently has a direct line to the woman I love.

"She's not doing well," Avery tells him, a tremor in her words. "Jared, I didn't realize how quickly she's been declining. I'm not ready to say goodbye to her."

My hands grip the steering wheel as I merge onto the freeway that will take us to Queens. A steady rain has begun, pattering against the roof. Under the relentless beat, I hear Jared offering Avery quiet comfort, indistinct reassurances that sound heartfelt and sincere. They talk for a few more minutes, her tone sober, thready with emotion. Then she quietly says goodbye, promising to call him again tomorrow.

"That was Jared."

"So I gathered." I sound annoyed, but I can't help it.

"He's going to check in on Kathryn in the morning and let me know how she is."

I nod, silent as we turn onto Avery's block in Forest Hills. The rain has picked up now, pelting the windshield and creating a pounding racket above our heads. I park on the street outside her house, but leave the car running.

"Come on. I'll see you to the door."

She starts to protest but I'm already climbing out from behind the wheel. I head around to her side and help her out, shrugging free of my suit coat to hold it over her head as we jog up the short walkway to her front door.

She turns to face me on the stoop, beneath the gabled overhang.

I'm suddenly glad for the noise of the rain. It fills the vacuum of everything I want to say to her right now. Possessive, demanding things that have no place here tonight.

That she is mine. That I can't wait another goddamn minute to know if I still stand a chance with her or if I've lost her forever. Or worse, could I lose her to a smooth player like Jared Rush?

I can't tell her that I'm losing my fucking mind without her. That what I want more than anything is to carry her up to her bed and take away all of the pain and fear and sorrow she's feeling, even if she'll only let me come back for this one night.

I'm not sure I've got the honor it's going to take to leave her right now. But to stay a moment longer is to take advantage of her vulnerability, her misplaced trust in me—something I've done plenty of already.

"Nick." Her eyes swim with unshed tears and confusion as she looks up at me.

I don't wait for her to say anything more. I don't

dare. "I have to go."

I press a brief, tender kiss to her parted lips. Then I dash back to my waiting car before I have the chance to change my mind.

11

I close the door and lean against it with a heavy sigh after Nick returns to his car.

What does it say about me that I can spend two hours looking after my terminally ill friend yet come home feeling sorry for myself when Nick practically ditches me at my front door? I feel adrift in my own house, left alone with just my thoughts and my worry for the friend I already feel slipping away from me.

It's too late at night to call Tasha or my mom, and when I phoned Lita from Kathryn's to update her on the situation, she informed me that she'd caught a cab home from the auction and was headed to bed.

That's where I should be heading too. That is, if I had any hope of going to bed and not lying there for the next several hours thinking about Nick.

Wanting him.

Needing the kind of contentment and comfort I've only ever felt in his arms.

I pick up my phone, my fingers itching with the urge to dial his number. I could ask him to come back. I know he would. I also know that if I'd invited him into my home tonight, into my bed, we'd be crossing a threshold with no turning back.

If we try to return to each other again and fail, it will be for the last time. For my own sake, for my sanity, it would have to be.

As much as I wish I had Nick's strength to lean on, I'm not sure I'm ready to face that much finality in one night.

Instead I head upstairs to take a shower and try to relax. A few minutes under the hot water soothes my tired muscles. It washes away the tears I refused to let fall in front of Kathryn.

What it doesn't soothe or wash away are my thoughts of Nick.

My longing to be with him.

Those feelings cling to me as I wrap myself in a short silk kimono and pad across my bedroom rug to draw the blinds. It's still pouring outside, rain pelting wetly against the windows and sweeping in waves over the street below.

The street where Nick's black BMW still sits parked at my curb.

"What the hell?"

He's here? When did he come back? Or did he ever go at all?

It doesn't matter. He's here. I step back from the window in surprise, swamped by a selfish elation I can't deny.

Then I'm racing down the stairs and out the front door, barefoot. Breathless.

Puddles on the pavement slosh against my feet as I round the front of the car to the driver's side. I pound the flat of my hand against the window, a single knock that brings Nick's head up sharply.

Our eyes meet through the water-streaked glass. He's sitting in the darkened car, the engine turned off. He scowls, his lips parting on a silent curse as currents of rain sluice off my nose and chin.

The door pops open. I step aside as he climbs out of the car, an apology in his gaze. "I couldn't leave. Damn it, I tried to, but—"

I don't give him the chance to finish. With my hands holding his face, I drag him down to meet my kiss. His answering groan is animal, filled with the same yearning that's coursing wildly through me.

We're drenched in seconds. His white dress shirt plasters against his broad shoulders and chest. My thin kimono practically melts around me. Neither of us seems notice or care. Nothing can cool the urgency of our kiss.

Nick's mouth moves hungrily over mine, our faces wet from the rain, our lips fused and fevered. His large hands hold me close to him, one palm splayed at my back, the other cradling my nape beneath the sodden tangle of my hair. His muscles flex, then in an instant he's pivoted, turning me around so that I'm pinned between the closed door of the BMW and the firm heat of his body. He crowds in closer, still kissing me madly, our bodies crushed together everywhere they can, melding my soft curves to his hard planes.

I moan with the need for deeper contact. There's no use trying to deny what he does to me. Just one kiss and I'm his for the taking already.

Again.

Always.

He says my name like a curse, muttering it harshly against my lips before he draws back to look at me. Desire blazes in his eyes and in the stark set of his jaw.

I see the question in his gaze. The warning.

I nod, the only response I'm capable of when my body is shivering under the deluge, my senses thrumming with the force of my need.

Nick kisses me again, hard and fast and heated. His fingers lace through mine and together we hurry back to the house. Dripping wet in the center of my little foyer, we barely make it to the steps leading upstairs before Nick wheels me around to face him, picking right up where we left off. He kisses me until I feel dizzy, until I am vibrating with arousal.

It's always been like this between us from the very beginning. Spark meeting tinder. Passion perpetually smoldering and once reignited, swiftly consuming everything in its path.

But it's not only lust that draws us together time and again.

It's a connection that goes deeper than that. Nick and I share a mutual need that no one else can fill. I feel it every time I look into his haunted eyes and see a piece of myself there. As strong and unbreakable as he is, I know there's a part of Nick that recognizes himself in me too.

I feel our connection now, when his gaze locks on mine and he begins to peel away my soaked kimono. He lowers his head and his mouth finds the curve of my bare neck and shoulder. My skin is cold, but it flares hot the instant his lips touch me. I shudder with unabashed need, curling my arms around him as his lips descend to my breasts. The wet scrap of my clothing falls away, taking the rest of the world and all of my other conscious thoughts with it.

God. How I need this. I need him.

Tonight there is the added fuel of our separation, all the nights and weeks and months that I've longed to feel Nick's hands on me again, his mouth on me . . . his hard, powerful body crushed against me, buried inside me.

In spite of everything we've been through, there is still this. There will always be this. I know it as surely as I see that same truth reflected in his stormy blue eyes. We will be drawn together like this always, even if it hurts.

Even if it destroys us.

Right now I don't care about any of that.

Right now, all I need is him.

Nick understands. There's no need for me to say the words. He doesn't have to tell me how deeply he craves this either.

My fingers struggle to unbutton his wet shirt. The custom-tailored white fabric is glued to his muscled arms and torso, slowing my quest to get at his naked skin. He seems just as impatient to have my hands on him. Yanking the tails loose from his pants, he rips open the front of the shirt with a sharp flex of his wrists. Mother-of-pearl buttons clatter to the hardwood like tiny pebbles.

His sigh is ragged when I touch him. On a low sigh, he drops his head back as I run my fingers over his bare chest and abdomen. When I drift lower, palming the steely ridge of his arousal, a rough moan rumbles at the back of his throat.

Gripping my hips, he drags me against him, the rain-dampened bespoke slacks pressing coolly to my nakedness. His pelvis grinds into mine. The pressure and the friction of his hard erection rotating against me makes my core clench greedily. His mouth captures the impatient sound I make, even as his hands clamp on to my backside and haul me deeper into his embrace.

He slides his palms down the outsides of my thighs.

The next thing I know, his hand is between them, teasing the wet seam of my body. My spine arcs when his fingers delve into the cleft of my sex. It's been so long. To think I'd nearly had myself convinced that any sexual impulse I had was snuffed out the day I left Paris.

It was only waiting for this. For Nick.

"Oh, God." I gasp, shuddering against him as his touch slides through my wetness, his thumb rolling deliciously, torturously, over my clit. Each stroke winds me tighter, driving me toward a pleasure I can neither slow down nor contain. I want to burrow my face into his chest, but Nick moves back, watching me. Studying every nuance of my response.

As always, I'm stripped bare under his gaze.

Because even after a year apart I am his.

My climax breaks over me without warning. I cry out with the intensity of it, with the staggering force of everything I still feel for Dominic Baine.

I open my eyes a moment later and find he's still watching, still searching my face. And between my quivering thighs, his fingers are still moving reverently inside me.

"Christ, Avery. You're so fucking beautiful when you come." His voice is ragged, tight with desire. With his free hand, he gently caresses my cheek and brow. "I want to be inside you."

I press against him, smiling up into his sober face. "I want it too, Nick."

"No. You don't understand." He withdraws his fingers from inside me, then lowers his forehead to rest against mine. "I want more than that. I want to be the only man you take inside you."

"You are." I hold his serious gaze, unable to pretend with him now. I can't lie by letting him think it's been easy for me without him. Not after everything he's told me.

All the lies and pretending we've done with each other are part of our past now. If we're going to move forward, there's no room for anything but the truth.

"There's been no one else since you, Nick."

He grunts. "So, Professor Nice Guy. He really isn't in the picture?"

I shake my head. "He never was, just like you said. I broke it off with Brandon the day you and I talked at the gallery."

"And Jared Rush?"

I frown at both the question and his jealous tone, although it shouldn't surprise me. When we were together, Nick all but forbade me to get close to the charming artist even though the two men were on friendly terms in the past.

"Jared and I are friends, that's all. That's all we'll ever be," I assure him. "There's been no other men since you, Nick. No one. Not once. Not in all this time."

I see the jolt of astonishment flash across his face. I

see the relief.

"Damn you for letting me think they could have been." He exhales, then mutters a quiet curse. "Do you know how badly I wanted to forget you? How many times I went to a bar or a party for the sole purpose of finding some nameless, faceless female that I could fuck instead of tormenting myself every waking moment with the thought of wanting you?"

I'm holding my breath as he talks, yanked unwillingly back to reality. I'm terrified of what he's going to tell me. I had no claim on him this past year, but if he confesses to screwing half the women in this city, I don't know what I'll do. I can't bar him from my heart that easily, but if he felt so little for me that he could do what he's describing, I don't know how I'll be able to look at him and not feel like I'm in love with a stranger.

He lifts my chin, forcing me to give him my full attention. "I wanted to be able to fuck you out of my head, Avery. Out of my heart. But I couldn't do it. I didn't want anyone else. I still don't."

Hope catches in my chest. "Then you didn't—"

"No one," he says, brushing his lips over mine. "Not once." A tender kiss to the side of my neck that makes my pulse race and my heart leap. "Not in all this time."

Joy surges inside me, along with renewed desire. I can't contain either one. Throwing my arms around his neck, I leap at Nick, my bare legs encircling his waist. Our mouths meet with abandon, with ferocious hunger.

He holds me aloft, his palms and forearms supporting my weight. And then suddenly we're in motion, ascending the staircase that leads to my bedroom on the second floor.

Nick's never been in my house before. Never been

in the queen-sized bed that seems very small as he sets me down on the edge of it and stands before me to finish undressing.

He strips with elegant efficiency while I watch with eager eyes and a watering mouth. He's so heart-stoppingly handsome I nearly forget to breathe. I know every muscled ridge and plane of his body, yet he's never looked more virile than he does now.

He pushes me down on the mattress, his body covering me. His weight on me is a comfort as much as it arouses me. I cling to him, arching beneath him and yearning to have him buried deep inside me.

He knows what he does to me, even now. A year of distance between us, yet he still knows just how to touch me, how to kiss me. His tongue delves deep into my mouth, thrusting and withdrawing, stoking the fire that's barely banked from the orgasm he gave me downstairs.

I want to kiss him all night, but Nick has other plans.

Moving down the length of my body with his wicked hands and mouth, he leaves a trail of fire along my neck and across my breasts, then down to the shallow dip of my belly. I moan with the bliss of it, my spine arching off the mattress as his trek continues downward. He pauses at my hip bone, tracing the delicate edge of it with his tongue.

"I've been dreaming of tasting you again for too long," he murmurs harshly, his breath rolling hot and heavy over my sensitive skin. "Open for me, baby."

I comply with a shivery exhalation, every nerve ending riveted on Nick and the pounding need that's pulsing between us. As soon as my thighs part, he sinks down between them.

"Oh, God."

The first fleeting lick of his tongue against my sex spirals through me like liquid fire. Then another kiss, one that lingers much longer, his tongue cleaving into my center, driving me to the brink of glorious madness. He finds my clit and the tender, unrelenting assault he wages on that tight bundle of nerves is almost my undoing.

But he knows just how much to give me and just when to retreat. This dance is a familiar one for us. Give and take. Submission and demand.

Nick is a master at everything when it comes to my pleasure. He knows precisely how to prolong my torment and when to set me free.

What I need right now is him inside me.

On a deep, approving growl he kisses my pussy once more, stroking and nipping, then drawing the tender bud of my clit against the hot, wet heat of his tongue.

His hooded gaze lifts to mine in wicked promise as he licks his lips, which now glisten with my juices. "As sweet and hot as I remember," he murmurs darkly.

He moves back up now, every inch of him hard and hungry and so very beautiful. I clutch the solid bulk of his shoulders as he covers me, propped on his fists on either side of me, his thighs wedged between mine. His cock has always been impressive, but tonight it looks immense.

"I'll try to take it slow, but—" His words cut off on a hissed curse. "I just have to be inside you, Avery."

"Yes. Now, Nick."

I reach up to him, tunneling my fingers into his silken black hair as he penetrates me. The invasion stretches me nearly to the point of pain, even though I can feel how rigidly he's holding on to his control.

"Ah, fuck," he grinds out through clenched teeth,

shuddering with the first deep thrusts. "You feel so damn good."

"So do you." I arch to take him fully, to meet every soul-shattering drive of his body into mine. "Nick, don't stop."

"Never."

His eyes are rooted on mine, refusing to let me go. I surrender completely to the tempo he sets for us, taking comfort in his control. I feel safe when we're together like this. I feel protected.

Even after everything we've been through, I feel cherished.

I open to his kiss, meeting his tongue with mine as he claims my mouth in a hotter, hungrier joining that leaves me feeling drunk with pleasure and need.

His name is a tremulous whisper on my lips as he increases his rhythm. Each long push goes deeper than the last, adding to the fire that's roaring back to life inside me. His mouth covers mine as the first jagged cry of my orgasm erupts from the back of my throat.

There is no mercy in him now, only need.

He rocks into me feverishly, violently. His body goes tense, shuddering with each rapid pound of his hips against mine.

"Ah, Christ, baby. I'm close. I need to come inside you."

I nod, beyond words now.

His release rips loose from him in a coarse shout and a violent buck of his body.

"*Avery.*" His arms hold me tight beneath him as he empties within me in wave after spasming wave. When he says my name again, he utters it like a mantra. Maybe a curse.

There is a part of me that recognizes what I've done here. The threshold I wasn't sure I was ready to cross has now been obliterated.

I don't know if Nick will hurt me again.

I only know that I need him. I needed this.

Tonight I needed us.

The look in his eyes tells me he does too.

And for now, that's enough.

12

It's just after daybreak when I open my eyes and realize Nick is gone.

Disappointment jolts me, sharper than I care to admit. I push myself up to a sitting position on the cool sheets, my chest gone suddenly hollow.

That is, until I see Nick's shirt draped with his dark suit pants over my reading chair in the corner. His polished black leather shoes are still here, too, parked neatly beside my dresser.

So, where is he?

A quick glance toward the adjacent bathroom tells me he's also taken the time to shower. Jesus, how hard had I slept? Granted, Nick and I spent much of the night making love. I lost count of the times one of us woke the other with the insatiable urge to begin all over again.

All I know is that my body is sore in several places, each tender ache a sensual reminder of everything I'd been missing since Nick and I had been apart.

I slip out of bed and pad into the bathroom to check my hair and brush my teeth. Water still beads on the glass enclosure of the shower. The humid air carries the faint vanilla fragrance of my soap and the fruity scent of my shampoo. There's something gratifying and familiar, even erotic, about the idea of Nick using my toiletries as if he lives here. I smile in the mirror, taking probably a bit too much satisfaction in my bedraggled, well-pleasured reflection.

After I freshen up at the sink and twist my hair into a hasty knot on top of my head, I snag Nick's shirt from the chair and slip it on. The crisp cotton is dry now, but there's no fixing the lack of buttons down the front of it. I smile with the memory, feeling playful and sexy as I roll the overlong sleeves up on my forearms and head out of the bedroom to look for Nick.

The low timbre of his voice carries out from the kitchen.

"I thought I made myself clear on this the last time we spoke." Although he's speaking quietly, there's no mistaking the irritation in his tone. No, he's pissed as hell. "Yes, I understand the situation and I don't give a damn. Then tell the son of a bitch I said as much. No. There's nothing more to say on the matter. You have my answer and it's final."

My steps halt just outside the room. I stand there silent, feeling awkward and uncertain if I should interrupt. He pivots at that same moment, perhaps sensing that he's no longer alone. His call is ended without a goodbye, then he sets his phone on the counter.

I feel my brow furrow. "Sorry. I didn't know you were on the phone. Everything all right?"

"Just some business I needed to handle." His mouth curves in a sinfully hot smile. "I hope I didn't wake you."

"No. I slept like a rock until a minute ago."

He's practically naked, dressed in just his black boxer briefs. Now that I'm seeing him in the daylight, he's leaner than I recall. But still fit and strong, every inch of him roped in honed muscle sheathed in flawless golden skin. Desire pulses in me just to look at him.

I drift toward him, drawn as ever by the magnetism of this man but also by the memory of another morning after—our first—following my unplanned sleepover in his penthouse. We'd ended up in the kitchen that day, too, with Nick clad only in boxer briefs and me feeling awkward and twitchy, eager to make my escape before I was tempted to fall any deeper under his spell. There had been no hope of avoiding that, even then.

He leans casually against the counter, allowing me to drink in my fill of him. "You're wearing my shirt."

"Yes. It was a very nice shirt too." I glance down at the open front that exposes as much of me as it covers. "Shame it's ruined."

"Ruined? Not from where I'm standing. It's never looked better." His blue eyes darken as he takes a handful of the finely loomed cotton in each hand and pulls me against him. His arousal is unmistakable, pressing shamelessly into my belly. "You look good enough to eat in my shirt. Or out of it."

He lowers his head to mine and kisses me, his lips warm and intent and unhurried. His hands slip down my sides and around to the loose hemline that skims the backs of my thighs. I moan into his mouth as he palms my ass, his fingers firm and possessive. His bare skin feels hot everywhere we touch, his hard erection grinding against me in a slow rhythm that only makes me crave more.

"Hungry?" He murmurs against my parted lips.

"God, yes."

"Good. So am I." He chuckles darkly. It's not until I open my eyes that I realize he's talking about food. With a smirk on his lips and an amused arch of his brows, he lifts his head from our kiss. "I thought I'd round up some breakfast for us. If you don't mind."

"You mean take over my kitchen?" I feign an affronted look. "That's rather bold of you, Mr. Baine."

"I seem to recall you like my cooking. Do I need to remind you I make a mean eggs Benedict?"

"I remember. But my pantry is a bit more pedestrian than yours. In this kitchen the breakfast specialty is scrambled eggs and toast."

He grins. "That would be great. Do you trust me enough for coffee duty?"

"Only if you know how to use a French press."

"Do I know how," he mutters. With a light smack on my backside, he releases me so I can go fetch what he'll need from the cabinets. He takes the glass carafe and coiled plunger from my hands with a smirk. "Ms. Ross, you're about to have the best cup of coffee of your life."

I laugh, finding it so natural to slip back into a state of normalcy with him. It's unnerving how effortless it is to banter and tease with him. Surreal to glance over and find him working beside me in my kitchen after spending most of the night in my bed upstairs making love.

I put the bread in the toaster, then busy myself at the stove with the pan of eggs while Nick comes over to retrieve the steaming teapot. After pouring hot water into the press on the counter, he comes back to replace the kettle on the extinguished back burner.

He lingers beside me, watching me grind salt and pepper on the eggs. "What are your plans for the day?"

"I want to look in on Kathryn this morning. If she's feeling well enough for company, I'd like to visit with her for a while." I nod in the direction of the cupboard next him. "Will you grab a couple of plates and mugs?"

He places the dishes on the counter. "Will you see Jared there today?"

"I don't know. Possibly." He grunts unhappily, but says nothing. I can't imagine how he could be worried about Jared or any other man after last night. But Nick is a possessive man, and I'd be lying to myself if I try to pretend I don't remember what it's like to be the recipient of all that primal male attention and focus. I glance at over at him, more amused than I should be. "How's the coffee situation?"

"Totally under control," he says without even checking. "What are your plans after you check on Kathryn?"

"I thought I'd go into the studio. I'm making good progress on a piece I hope to finish this week, but I'm also hoping to see Lita. She said something to me at the event last night that's been bothering me."

"Lita, your friend who'd caught the eye of Derek Kingston."

"That's right," I say, struck by the fact that he remembers a conversation he and I had more than a year ago about my friend and the former rockstar. "But it was her art that caught his eye."

Nick smiles. "I'm sure it was. What did the asshole do to her?"

"I don't know. Whatever it was, it was bad enough to make her walk off the project yesterday." I turn the flame off the pan of cooked eggs, then butter the toast that popped while we were talking. "Lita's been living and breathing that project for months. I've never seen her so consumed by anything else she's worked on before, yet suddenly she just decides to quit?"

"The guy's got a reputation for being difficult," Nick says. "I'm sorry if your friend got the brunt of it."

"Me too. I just want to make sure she's okay."

He nods, considering. "And after you do that, what's next on your list for the day?"

"I don't know."

"Then come out with me."

"Out with you," I say, tilting my head at him. "Are you asking me out on a date?"

"I'm trying to." The edge of his mouth quirks. "A bit out of sequence, considering last night, but, yes, Avery, I'd like to take you out. On a proper date."

"What time?"

"You decide. You can call me later today and let me know when you'll be free."

"What if I decide to stay late at the studio?"

"I'll wait."

Then, as if the matter has been decided, he walks over to work the coffee press and fill our mugs. Without having to ask me, he adds both cream and sugar to mine—just the way I like it—and hands the mug to me.

I take a sip and damn if he wasn't right. It's as if I've never tasted good coffee before. "Oh, my God. This really is the best coffee I've ever had."

With a told-you-so shrug, he clinks his mug against mine. "Trust, Ms. Ross."

It's a teasing remark, but we both feel its significance too. How many times did Nick say those very words to me after we first met? How often did he press me for honesty and trust, even though he knew all along that he wasn't giving me the same thing?

Reckless.

That's what I was with him the first time. There's a part of me that fears I'm stepping into the same snare now, getting too comfortable too quickly. Justifying the pain we've both caused each other because of the pleasure we take in being together.

There is something dangerously comfortable about the way it feels to slip back into our old habits as if the past year hadn't happened. As if last night has erased it all and we're back together again.

It's unsettling how much I want to believe that we can simply pick up and resume what we had. Terrifying how quickly my heart is ready to let him back in.

I set my mug down, then pivot away from him to serve our far-from-gourmet breakfast. Nick moves in behind me, brushing his knuckles tenderly along my cheek.

"You've gotten quiet. You okay?" When I only nod, he puts his mug on the counter next to mine, then turns me around to face him. He's scowling, but it's not anger I see in his eyes. "If this is going too fast for you . . . If it's uncomfortable having me here, tell me. I'll go."

"No. It's not that. And I don't want you to go."

"Then what?" He sounds truly worried, as if I'm the one with the power to wound him. "Avery, if you think last night was a mistake—"

"It wasn't." I sigh, shaking my head. "Last night felt too good to be a mistake. All of this, being with you again like this . . . it feels too good to be a mistake."

"Because it isn't." His tone is as resolute as his touch is gentle. He cradles my face in his palms, searching my gaze. "I won't let this be a mistake. Not this time. Not if you can forgive me for what I've done."

"I did some awful things too. I lied to you about a lot of things and you forgave me."

"Yes. Because I understood you kept all those things from me in order to protect yourself. From your past. From the people who could still hurt you. And, yes, even from me." His thumb traces my lips. "I forgave you because I loved you, Avery. I still do. Christ, I would do anything for you."

I close my eyes for a moment, letting the words sink in.

"Tell me you believe me," he says quietly.

"I believe you, Nick." I brush my fingers through his inky black hair, helpless to keep from touching him. "And I love you too."

He breathes out, a sound of relief. Of hope. "Can you forgive me?"

"I already have."

"But you don't trust me."

"I want to, Nick." My mind crowds with all of the reasons I have to be careful, to be wary around him now. We both came to each other via deception, no matter how either of us needs to rationalize our actions or justify our motivations. We both have our excuses. We have our demons to be slayed. But if this is going to work—if we stand any chance of lasting—then we have to rebuild on a foundation of truth.

"Avery, tell me what I need to do."

"No more secrets. No more games or power plays." I shake my head, realizing my ultimatum could end this even before it begins again. But it's the only way. Anything less would already be a lie. "I need honesty from you this time, Nick. You need to let me in. You need to trust me. If you can't give me that—"

"I can," he says, his voice intense with emotion. "Anything, Avery. I'm not going to lose you again."

"You'd better mean that."

He nods solemnly. "Every word."

Then he kisses me, gathering me close and holding me there for the longest time. When we separate I look up into ocean blue eyes that have gone stormy with desire. The same desire that's smoldering inside me.

Nick kisses me again, slow and deep.

He pushes his shirt off my shoulders and it drops onto the checked tile of my kitchen floor.

Our breakfast will be cold, but I don't care. I can't even mourn the phenomenal cup of coffee I won't be drinking after all.

Not when I have Nick's promise to hold on to and his arms wrapped around me.

Right now there is nothing more I need.

13

I'm still thinking about Avery when my personal attorney Andrew Beckham walks into my office and sets a stack of contracts and a rolled up blueprint on my desk.

I glance at the cover page on the papers, then look up at Beck. "The deal on the Australian high-rise cleared?"

He nods, looking smugly confident. "You told me to look for cracks in the regulatory code that were obstructing the sale. Well, I found one."

Intrigued, I lean back in my chair as he takes a seat on the other side of the desk from me. I've worked with Beck for years, consider him my best friend in many ways. With his rich brown skin and arresting pale green eyes, he's the kind of guy who turns female heads every time he walks in the room. But behind the knife-edge cheekbones and smooth-as-silk smile is one of the sharpest minds I've ever encountered.

Fortunately for me, he works for Baine International.

"The current tower already exceeds new height restrictions that were passed a few years ago," he explains. "Because we're planning extensive renovations and expansion of the existing footprint, our request to be grandfathered in under the old regulation was denied."

"Which is why we agreed we wouldn't build up," I remind him. "But our team on the ground in Melbourne seemed pretty convinced last night in our conference call that our hands were going to be tied on any kind of expansion."

"They were right." Beck's mouth starts to curve, lifting the corners of his trim goatee. "But we can sidestep the regulations if we incorporate a new community area into our plans."

I frown, already considering our options. "You're talking about building a small park or playground for the building?"

Beck nods. "It'll add to the overall cost of the project, but we'll recoup it in less than ten years simply based on the current building revenue. Plus, we'll be improving the quality of life for the residents."

"Good work." I pick up my pen and scribble my signature on the agreements. "Now we just have to figure out how to make it happen."

He chuckles. "You mean you have to figure it out. I just connect dots and push paper, my friend."

We both pause when my assistant, Lily Fontana,

appears in the open doorway. "Excuse me for interrupting. Nick, there's a job foreman from a YMCA construction site in New Jersey on the phone. He says he just received a shipment of drawer pulls and cabinet knobs delivered to him and he's not sure what to do with them."

Beck and I exchange a confused look. "Why's he calling us?"

"Because the shipment is addressed to you. It was supposed to be delivered to the recreation center job site. The supplier sent it to the wrong place."

"What do we have on site now?"

Lily's face blanches a little. "Um, nothing. I checked with our site foreman before I bothered you. Rudy says no one realized the parts hadn't arrived yet. Someone checked them off the punch list by mistake."

I don't hold back the harsh curse that rips off my tongue. The rec center is the first thing I've actually built from the ground up, not acquired and improved or torn down to start again. It's personal. More important to me than anything I've ever done in business before.

So even a minor fuck up like this matters.

"Have Rudy order the parts again. I'll pick them up myself if I have to."

"He's already tried to get some more delivered. They're on backorder. They won't be in until next month."

"Unbelievable. More than a million in kitchen equipment installed in that place but no one bothered to look at the cabinets? Jesus Christ." I rake a hand over my head. "Tomorrow we're going to have a couple dozen reporters out there on a private press tour ahead of the ribbon-cutting in a few days. Are you telling me there's a chance we won't have any hardware on the drawers or cabinets?"

"I'll go pick them up from the New Jersey location," Lily offers.

"No. That's all right," I tell her. Even though she's always willing to go above and beyond, this is my problem to handle. "I'll make sure the parts get to the site. I want to walk through again by myself before the press descends on the place anyway."

She frowns. "Sorry, Nick."

"Not your fault." No, it's mine. I should have been monitoring the progress more closely. The truth is, I've had one primary concern for the past week or so and that's Avery. Although I'd only be lying to myself if I try to pretend my head has been fully in the game for the entire past year. "Thank you, Lily. I'll handle this."

"Okay. I'll text you the address."

She retreats to her desk and a few seconds later, her message hits my phone.

"Anything I can do?" Beck asks as he takes the signed contracts and slides them into a folder.

"Yeah." I slant him a wry look as I stand up. "Be ready with bail money in case I discover any other disasters when I get to the rec center site."

He chuckles as he pivots and heads out the door.

"Hey, you think I'm joking?"

I step out from behind my desk to retrieve my suit jacket from the closet. I'm shrugging into it when my cell phone chimes. No need to look at the screen before my dark mood starts to lift. It's Avery's ring tone, the one I set for her more than a year ago. The one I never had the heart to delete in all the time we'd been apart.

"Hello, beautiful." There is a pause on the other end

of the line. "Avery?"

"Hi." Another pause, followed by her quiet laugh. "I think it's going to take a little time for me to get used to hearing your voice in my ear. Especially hearing you say that."

It's how I often greeted her when she'd call me, and it feels astonishingly normal to be doing so again. I nod to Lily as I walk past her desk on my way out to the elevator.

"Where are you at?"

"The studio. I got here a few minutes ago."

I glance at my watch and push the button for the executive garage. It's still early in the day, not yet eleven o'clock. I dropped her off at Kathryn's around nine. "How did things go this morning?"

"Kathryn was awake when I got there. She sat up in bed for a while and we talked for about forty-five minutes before she started nodding off." I hear the optimism in Avery's voice, but I also hear the concern. "Pauline, her nurse, told me she's refusing to take her pain meds today. Kathryn says they only make her want to sleep more. We already know how she feels about missing out on anything."

I grunt in acknowledgment. "That's one thing that'll never change."

"I hope it won't," she says, going quiet and somber on me. "The minute Kathryn stops caring that she's not at the center of all the action I'll know it's time to brace myself for the worst."

She's right about that. I exit the descended elevator and wake my car with a jab of the remote. The black M6 chirps in its parking spot near the lift. "Have you had a chance to talk to your sculptor friend? I'm curious to hear what went wrong with Derek Kingston."

Although I'm reluctant to bring up yet another worry of hers, I'd rather steer Avery away from fears of Kathryn's furthering decline. Hell, there are countless things I'd rather talk about other than disease and dying too.

"What went wrong?" Avery seems to choke a bit on the answer. "They slept together."

"Ah, Christ." I climb behind the wheel of my car and start the engine. Then I hit the hands-free, putting Avery on the speakers. Hearing her voice surround me is a pleasure I want to savor. "Didn't I tell you when she met the guy that she wouldn't want to get involved with him?"

"Yes, you did. The same way a lot of people I know tried to warn me about you."

I scowl into my rearview mirror as I back out of the parking space. Although I had to concede the point to her on that one, it didn't mean I had to agree. "Our situation is different. You and I are different."

"She's in love with him, Nick. I don't think she realizes it yet, but I can tell. I can see it in her eyes when she talks about him. Even when she's insisting he's the most aggravating man she's ever met."

"Maybe I need to have a talk with Kingston, one on one," I suggest. "Make sure he understands that if he hurts this woman he'll have to answer to me. Say the word and I'll head out to Brooklyn Heights right now."

She laughs. "Don't you dare! Besides, you won't find him at Dektech's headquarters. He just left the studio with Lita. They went somewhere to talk. At least, that's what they said they were going to do. Personally, I think they've got other plans than just talking."

"Sounds good to me. What are your plans for the rest of the day?"

"I don't know." I can feel the smile in her voice. "You got any ideas?"

"Hundreds of them." Even as I speak, I'm already ignoring the GPS route toward New Jersey, heading instead for Avery's studio in East Harlem. "I'll pick you up in fifteen minutes."

14

W hen you said you wanted to take me out on a proper date today, Nick, I have to admit I wasn't picturing kitchen hardware and Hoboken, New Jersey."

I slant a glance at Avery in the passenger seat as we near the end of the Lincoln Tunnel on our way back into the city. She's wearing the same flowy white off-the-shoulder top and denim shorts she had on when we left her house this morning, her silky blonde hair loose around her shoulders. She looks ethereal sitting beside me as we emerge from the tunnel and sunlight through the windshield bathes her in an angelic glow.

My angel. A miracle I know I damn well don't deserve.

I can't resist reaching across to touch the velvety

curve of her cheek. "We'll take care of the proper date tonight. This is just an errand I needed to run."

She arches a slender brow. "I didn't realize Dominic Baine, corporate titan, personally runs his own errands."

"I do when it matters."

"And a case of brushed stainless steel drawer pulls and cabinet knobs is one of those times that it matters?"

"Absolutely."

"Interesting."

I grin. "Got you wondering, don't I?"

She doesn't give me the satisfaction of an answer, but I see the little smirk she tries to keep from me as she looks out the window at the passing landscape of the city. Eventually, we turn onto Twenty-fifth in Chelsea and head toward a residential block where clusters of tan brick apartment buildings flank both sides of the busy street.

Situated between a group of them on a section of the neighborhood where a couple of eyesore tenement relics from the Sixties used to stand is a brand-new construction brick-and-glass complex with a small parking area on the side of it.

I see Avery frown, studying the building and the banner announcing the grand opening later this week. She pivots around to face me, a look of delight dancing in her beautiful green eyes.

"Oh, my God. Nick, this is the youth recreation center. *Your* rec center."

When I first told her about my plans for the project, it had been little more than sketches and schematics on paper. A dream I'd been trying to make happen for a couple of years before I met her. "Would you like to go inside and have a look?"

Her entire face lights up. "Yes!"

I park, then ditch my suit coat in the backseat and grab the box of hardware, tucking it under my arm as we head toward the entrance. Avery's practically bouncing with enthusiasm by the time it takes me to unlock the door and let her in.

As I shut the door behind us, she wades ahead of me into the spacious lobby, her long tan legs carrying her to the center of the room. Her head swivels from the gleaming floor inlaid with motivational quotes about overcoming adversity, to the open rafters of the ceiling festooned with hanging kites that look like wind-filled sails, to the painted mural that runs the entire length of the walls that will greet everyone who enters the center.

I watch her take in everything, all of the details I personally selected and oversaw. When she glances back at me, it's as if my pride is hers too. "This is incredible, Nick. This place, it's all you, isn't it?"

I shrug casually, only because inside me something soft, something alarmingly vulnerable, squeezes tight at her praise. I clear my throat and point toward the mural that's a bright tangle of trees, flowers, animals, and people, all of it connected by a joyful randomness of color and abstract flourishes. "We brought in kids from the surrounding neighborhoods to paint this. I wanted the community to understand this center belongs to them, not me."

Avery's voice is quiet with unabashed wonder. "This is amazing, Nick. It's perfect."

"Not quite." I jiggle the box of kitchen hardware. "Just one last thing to take care of. Come on, I'll show you around."

I bring her through the central lobby into the large

gymnasium. Benches surround the regulation-size basketball court, which is outfitted with multiple hoops. Rolling carts filled with a dozen brand-new balls stand in one corner. In the other is a collection of wrestling mats and volleyball nets.

Avery takes one of the basketballs off the cart and bounces it a few times, grinning at me. "Think we could come and watch the kids play sometime?"

I chuckle. "Sure. For a second I thought you were going to ask me to throw down with you right here and now."

"Afraid I'd beat you?"

"Only if I have to play with one hand holding on to this box at the same time."

She laughs. "That sounds like a challenge, Mr. Baine."

"If you're not careful, it will be." I swipe the ball in mid-bounce, palming it and setting it back on the cart. "There's more to see. Come along, Ms. Ross."

We exit the gym through the back door near the lockers and fully equipped fitness room. Heading up the corridor, I show her the center's six-lane swimming pool and another room that will be used for aerobics and yoga classes.

She glances up at me as we move through one empty area to the next. "Are we the only ones here today? I don't see any workers."

I nod. "Finish construction wrapped up a few days ago. Except for one or two final punch list items, everything's in place and waiting for the ribbon-cutting this week. Tomorrow there'll be some folks from the media coming through for photos and press releases, but right now we have the whole place to ourselves."

She smiles. "You mean we could skinny-dip in the pool and no one would be the wiser?"

My cock stirs to swift, full attention. "We might want to make sure the security cameras are turned off first."

I indicate the small black devices mounted high in the corners of the corridor and the activity rooms. Avery laughs and waves at the one above our heads.

"Come on, I'll show you the rest." I place my free hand at the small of her back. Then I lean down until my lips brush her ear. "We'll return to your very excellent idea about getting naked after the tour."

We move on to the second floor, which houses a computer lab and library as well as study rooms where latchkey kids and other youth in need of somewhere to go will find comfortable chairs and quiet areas for homework or just a place to get away.

Avery soaks it all in, looking at me with wonderment in her soft gaze and her voice. "I've never seen anything like this."

She hasn't hidden her enthusiasm at all since we began our tour, nor does she seem the least bit bored as I've pointed out the minutiae of various building details and the many activities the center will provide.

We're paused in one of the cozy study rooms when she exhales a tender sigh and lays her hand against the side of my face. "Do you have any idea what a gift you've created for this community? You've done something truly remarkable here, Nick."

Her approval touches me more deeply than I'm prepared for. Even though we weren't together to share in the actual construction of the rec center, touring it with her now feels as though she is a part of it with me. It feels natural and right that she and I should share this together, just the two of us.

I kiss her, savoring her kindness and the sweet taste of her. How I managed to go the entire year without the feel of her lips against mine, I have no idea. It's not easy to break the contact. Harder still to put the thought of making love to her out of my mind when all I want to do is drop the box in my hand and bury myself inside her right here where we stand.

But I wasn't joking about the cameras. They're installed for the safety of the center's patrons as much as they're in place for insurance requirements.

I groan and force myself to draw away from her delectable mouth.

"Do you want to see more?" My voice is gravel in my throat, all of my blood vacated from my head to the massive bulge straining the zipper of my suit pants.

"I want to see everything you're prepared to show me, Mr. Baine."

I chuckle and take her hand in mine. As we ride the elevator back down to the main floor, I try to distract myself with the tour guide spiel I'll be reciting for the press tomorrow. "Beyond athletics and study, we'll also have creative classes for the kids. Dance, drama, art."

"Sounds great," she says as we alight from the lift.

I nod. "We'll also have a gourmet chef on hand to cook meals for the kids who need them and to instruct the ones who want to learn their way around a kitchen."

Avery's brows rise as I bring her to a pair of swinging doors and push them open. She stares for a moment, then on a gasp she walks past me into the industrial-size professional kitchen designed to my personal specifications.

"Holy shit."

She strolls by the multitude of stainless steel gas ranges, grill tops, ovens, and prep counters that dominate one entire side of the kitchen. On another side of the massive room is a walk-in freezer with more square footage than most of the apartments in this neighborhood, and a wall of built-in refrigerators with food storage space ample enough to feed an army.

I set the box of hardware down on a nearby counter and follow behind her as she peruses every square inch of the place. "I thought all of this gleaming metal might seem cold and clinical to the kids who come in here, so I had a craftsman come out and build all of the teak cabinetry and pantry shelving."

She walks over to it, running her fingers lightly over the clean lines of a cupboard. Then she lets out a soft exhalation and shakes her head. "There's no way to open any of these cabinets or drawers."

I lift my shoulder, my smile sardonic. "Do you know your way around a screwdriver?"

She grins back at me. "I think I can manage."

"Good. You're hired."

I go and fetch a hand drill and the other things we'll need from a toolbox stowed in the janitorial closet, then Avery and I set to work measuring and installing the hardware.

It feels good to have her next to me, completing something as a team. She's careful and exacting, her eye for detail even more meticulous than mine. But it's not just Avery's nature that makes her treat this simple task as if it's the most important thing in the world.

She's doing it for me.

I see that truth in her gaze when we finish the last drawer and stand back to look at our completed job.

What I see in her eyes humbles me. It staggers me.

Makes me love her more than I had even before.

"Look at what you've done, Nick." Her warm smile reaches deep inside me, to a place no one has ever touched before. Not before her. "It's incredible, all of it. I know how much the rec center means to you. I remember how important it was to you to see this vision come to life and you did it."

My chest tightens inexplicably at her praise because she understands this isn't just another construction project to me. Not another business I could consume and reinvent in an effort to turn an easy profit. This is different.

This is a piece of me.

"You created something that's going to have a lasting influence on this entire community and on every child who comes through its doors."

I nod, but the movement feels tight.

This is more than an altruistic gesture for this community that's many miles away from the dirt roads and swamps of my youth. I built this for myself too.

This building is the place I longed for when I was a troubled boy with problems too big for me to handle. It's the sanctuary where I wished I could have gone when every other part of my life was spiraling horrifically out of control. When I felt I had no one to turn to and nowhere to go.

Avery doesn't understand everything I was running from as a kid—the monsters I've buried deep in my past—but when I look into her searching eyes right now, I know that she can see the fissures in my veneer. She sees past the suits and the cars and the wealth.

Hell, I think she always has, right from the start.

Her hands are tender when she reaches up to hold my face. Her gaze captures mine, refusing to let go. Pleading with me to let her in.

"Thank you for bringing me here. For letting me share this with you." She smiles, those gentle eyes killing me with the depth of emotion I see in them. "I'm happy for you, that this all came together the way you dreamed it would. But it's more than that, Nick. I'm proud of you."

The words hit me hard. I can't recall the last time I heard someone say them to me.

And never the way Avery is saying them now.

I've never seen the kind of love that's shining at me from the light in her eyes.

Suddenly I can't find my voice, not that I even know how to respond. On a growl, I pull her into my arms, hoping my kiss will tell her all the things I'm unable to articulate right now.

The good and the bad.

Even the sickening things no one else knows—no one who ever cared about me, that is.

Like a wave gaining strength as it races toward the shore, the impulse to let her in—to open the door just a crack and see if she'll stand fast or run away—nearly overwhelms me.

I'm not sure if I'm ready to test her like that.

I can't imagine a day that I ever will be.

When I lift my head from our kiss, my breath is sawing out of me, my heart hammering in my temples.

Her brow furrows as she holds my gaze. "What's wrong?"

I shake my head, unwilling to ruin the day we just shared by inviting her sympathy. Or, Christ, her pity.

That's something I never want to see in her eyes.

But I already am ruining it all. My silence is making her anxious.

She takes a step back, out of my arms. "Where did you go just now, Nick?" She studies me, uncertainty creeping into her quiet voice. "You got so quiet. Was it something I said?"

"What?" My response comes out harsh, incredulous. "No. You didn't say anything wrong."

"Then talk to me."

I look away from her and curse low under my breath. I'm fucking this up and I know it. But damn it, the words won't come. They stay stuffed halfway down my throat, foul and unmoving.

Her expression sags in my lengthening silence.

When her phone abruptly starts ringing, we both flinch.

It bleats three times before she reaches into her purse to retrieve it. "It's Pauline," she murmurs woodenly. "I gave her my number this morning and asked her to call if anything changed today."

I nod, feeling absurd as I stand there, our sudden impasse stalled as she takes the call.

Avery's face blanches a second after she says hello. She hangs up a moment later. "I need to go to the hospital. Kathryn's in an ambulance on the way to the ICU."

15

Nick holds my hand as we get off the elevator on the intensive care floor of the hospital.

Because we're not family of Kathryn's, the staff at the nursing station can tell us nothing about her condition. Instead they direct us to a waiting room that's filled with other anxious and grieving people. Nick and I take the only two vacant seats next to each other. And then we wait, sandwiched between a set of parents trying to reassure their fearful children that their grandpa will be home again once his heart is better, and a middle-aged man with tear-stained cheeks staring zombie-like at the muted flat screen television while he absently twists the worn gold wedding band on his finger.

Although there is a heavy swinging door that separates the seating area from the ICU corridor outside, there's no escaping the constant jarring barrage of hospital noise and activity. Intercom announcements summon doctors and other personnel. Nursing staff moving occupied gurneys and wheelchairs tethered to IV poles and medical equipment sail past the narrow window of the waiting room in a seemingly never-ending parade.

Each time I hear the sudden piercing alarm ring out from a patient's room outside, my throat constricts with panic.

"I wish they'd let us see her."

Nick wraps his arm around my shoulders and presses a kiss to my temple. "I'm sure they'll tell us something soon."

Although he sounds confident and his embrace is warm and tender, when I look at him I'm not sure he actually sees me. There is a tension around his mouth that I haven't witnessed before. His mood has been grim since we left the rec center. Each mile that brought us closer to the hospital seemed to make him withdraw a little more.

And I haven't forgotten the odd silence that had engulfed him even before then.

I swivel my head to look at his unreadable profile. "Is everything okay?"

His eyes meet mine and I know he understands what I'm really asking. *Are you okay? Are we?*

"Yes." His expression is utterly earnest. In Nick's solemn, honest gaze, I feel our connection as strongly as ever. He's giving me that now, trying to let me in. Tenderly, he draws my hand to him, linking our fingers. "I'm here with you, baby. Don't ever doubt that. I'm not going anywhere."

I want to believe that. And I don't doubt he cares about me, or even that he might love me as completely, as desperately, as I love him. But there are times when I feel Nick is always just a hairbreadth out of my reach, existing somewhere no one can ever truly touch him.

It's that part of him I fear the most. The part that makes me worry if I hold on too tightly, probe too deeply, he'll be gone.

I recognize that elusiveness in him because I've spent most of my life in that place too.

The waiting room door swings open and Kathryn's personal nurse nods at Nick and me in greeting. She gestures for us to join her in the hall outside.

"She's stabilized," Pauline assures us right away. "She was in one of her stubborn moods and refused to take her afternoon pain medicines. I'm her nurse and she pays me to take care of her, but I can't hold her down and force her to swallow those pills."

"No. Of course, not."

She lets out a regretful sigh. "Twenty minutes later, I found her out on the terrace, slumped on one of the chairs. I can't be certain how long she'd been there, but she wouldn't respond and her blood pressure was bottoming out, so I immediately called 911."

Nick curses low under his breath. "You say she's all right now?"

"As best as can be expected, considering the progression of her disease," Pauline offers gently. "The doctors are administering IV fluids and pain medications. They'll monitor her here in ICU overnight most likely, then reevaluate her tomorrow."

Relieved somewhat, at least temporarily, I swallow the knot of dread that had been sitting in my throat since we arrived. "Can we see her now?"

Tapping a code into the keypad at the entrance of the secured intensive care wing, Pauline brings us past room after room of patients in various states of trauma or illness. Nick still holds my hand as we walk, our fingers threaded together. His grip is firm, and I don't miss the subtle tightening of his grasp as we make our way deeper into the ICU.

Pauline pauses outside the door to Kathryn's dimly lit room. "She's been sleeping on and off for a bit. Stay as long you like. If she wakes up, I know she'll be happy to see familiar faces."

She leaves us then, explaining that she needs to speak with Kathryn's oncologist. Nick and I quietly enter the room. He directs me to the cushioned vinyl recliner in the corner while he seems to prefer to stand, ignoring the metal guest chair situated at the foot of the bed. For a long time, we simply wait amid the steady beep and hiss of monitors.

I notice Nick has hardly looked at Kathryn since we came in. His gaze darts aimlessly from one thing in the room to another. Never at the bed or the machines. Never at her lying so still on the bed. He once cared for Kathryn enough to be her lover for a time and although they had their falling out years ago, I don't expect it's easy for him to see her like this.

Resting on the elevated mattress, she looks pale and dramatically frailer than when I saw her just this morning. Her steel-gray hair is thin and matted against her skull, her cheeks sallow and gaunt. An oxygen tube rides under her nose, and taped to the back of her hand and the bend of her elbow are IV lines running from multiple bags hanging from the pole at her bedside.

She stirs, moaning softly in her drugged sleep.

At her sudden agitation, Nick begins to pace silently near the door while I go to her side and gently comb her hair with my fingers.

"It's okay, Kathryn," I tell her, despite that she probably can't hear me. I need to say the words in case she can. "You just rest, now and feel better."

When I glance at Nick, I find him watching me. There is a heartbreaking tenderness in his eyes but there is also pain. There is an anxiety about him that he is struggling to keep clamped up tight, yet I see it in the careful set of his jaw. I feel it in the grim tension that's practically rolling off him where he stands.

Good Lord. He is miserable in this room—in this place. And while I know he understands the gravity of Kathryn's condition, I sense his distress is coming from a deeper place.

When Pauline appears at the door and quietly enters, he jolts at the intrusion.

"Avery, can I speak to you in the hall for a moment?"

My gaze slides to Nick for a second, but if he feels at all reluctant to stay behind in the room, he doesn't let on.

No, all I see in his face now that we're not alone is calm control and confidence. I see the facade of cool detachment that Dominic Xavier Baine presents to the world. The one he presented to me in the beginning, too, before I learned to see past it.

But have I really?

The question clings to me as I follow Kathryn's nurse out to the corridor.

16

A hissed curse gusts out of me the instant Avery exits the room.

Jesus. Get a fucking grip.

Bad enough I nearly pussied out in front of her at the rec center with some pathetic sob story about my less than perfect childhood. Now this?

I don't realize I'm pacing again until I glance out the window and see her looking my way while she speaks with Kathryn's private nurse. It's the only thing that halts my steps—that look that says she's just as concerned about me as she is the friend who's slowly perishing day by day before her eyes.

I know she senses my discomfort in being in this godforsaken place.

I hate that I can't hide that from her the way I can

with anyone else.

No, Avery knows me too well. And if I don't pull my shit together, I'm only going to add undue worry to an already painful day for her.

I force myself to take a seat in the metal guest chair at the foot of the bed. Try to tune out the noise of the monitors beeping with Kathryn's vitals and the various diagnostics that run automatically from a computer hooked up to wires and lines attached to various parts of her diseased body.

I tell myself not to think about another hospital room, and another frail, deteriorating body.

But the memories are already resurrected. They've been haunting me ever since Avery and I arrived.

"Are you gonna die, Mom?"

"Oh, honey." Sad, dove-gray eyes look up at me where I stand at the side of her hospital bed. "That's the last thing I want you to worry about. I'm sick, but I'm fighting this with all I've got. You believe me, don't you, sweetheart?"

I nod, but I'm not sure what I believe. She's never lied to me before, but each time I've come to see her in this place she looks smaller. Weaker. As if she's disappearing breath by breath.

Her fingers feel cool when she rests them on mine. Dark blue veins spider across the back of her hand, old bruises from IV lines mottling the skin that used to be creamy golden-brown from days spent in the Florida sun.

She turns her head on the mound of pillows that prop her up in the bed, the sparse post-chemo cap of fuzzy mahogany hair reminding me of a baby bird I once tried to rescue after it fell out of its nest. I couldn't save that bird. I woke up one morning and found it stiff and cold in the shoebox I fashioned for its cage.

Mom glances at the backpack slung over my shoulder, which I've carried here straight from school. "Do you have something to show me today?"

"Yeah." I reach into my pack, fishing around the books and homework from my fourth grade classes until I find the large spiral pad secreted at the bottom. I open to the page I made for her today and tear the pencil sketch out.

I don't want to notice the way her hands tremble as she holds it. Her graceful, artist's hands, almost too weak to hold a single sheet of drawing paper now. Her eyes mist as she gazes at my work for a long time.

"Oh, Nicky. It's beautiful."

I want to lean toward her, yearning to be close, but I stay still. I don't like the odor of antiseptics that hovers around her, nor the faint ammonia tinge from the tube that runs from beneath her blanket into the bag of dark yellow fluid hanging near my feet.

When she looks at me with pride beaming in her eyes, I feel ashamed of my discomfort in being near her. I should be stronger than this.

I should be brave, but all I am is afraid.

"This is your best one yet, sweetheart." Her cracked lips spread in a tender smile. *"Do you have any idea how special you are, how talented you are?"*

I shrug, aware even at ten years old that she's the talented one. Or she was, until the cancer took all of that away from her a few months ago.

"Promise me you'll keep at it, Nicky. You have to. You're too gifted to let a gift like this go to waste."

"Dad doesn't like it when I work on my art."

I sound sullen, but I can't help it. He and I have never gotten along. We never do things together, which is okay with me because when we do he just seems angry with me. Sometimes I think he can't even stand the sight of me.

"Dad says art is for girls. And sissy boys."

She scoffs, an airless sound that seems to scrape her throat.

"He doesn't mean that. Your father had a hard life, honey. His life is still hard, trying to support the three of us with what little he and your grandpa bring in from the boat."

A boat he refuses to let me step foot on. I'm too young, he says. Too soft for his line of work. Always mocking me.

He doesn't know what I'm capable of because he's never there to watch me try.

"He loves you, sweetheart. Don't ever doubt that."

I nod and smile, if only to let her continue to believe that. A question burns in the pit of my stomach. A selfish one that leaps off my tongue before I can bite it back. "What am I going to do when you're gone?"

"My sweet boy." She lets my sketch fall against her sunken breast as she reaches for me. Her fingers grasp mine in a firm hold now, her gray eyes stormy with resolve. "I'm not going to leave you. I'm going to fight this and get better. Then I'll be home and everything will be back to normal again."

When I start to cry, she gently tugs me down, gathering my head to her shoulder. Then I don't care about the smells or the sounds of the many machines that are connected to her. I weep like the sissy boy my father thinks I am, terrified of losing everything I love—and the only person who's ever loved me.

"You'll see," she whispers as she kisses the top of my head. "I'm going to beat this stupid cancer. I'm going to get out of this hospital and then you and I are going to turn that old shed out back into our studio, how about that? We're going to draw and paint whenever we want to, just you and me. Is that a deal?"

I nod shakily, my tears slowing under the ferocity of her resolve. "Yeah. It's a deal."

"Everything's going to be all right, Nicky. I promise."

In the end, it was a promise she couldn't keep. She didn't get better. She didn't ever come home.

And after the cancer took her later that same month

and she was gone, my life at home became the worst kind of hell.

Then nothing was all right ever again.

"Dominic?"

The raspy voice startles me out of the past. My head snaps up to find Kathryn staring at me from where she lay on the bed. She licks her lips as if her mouth is too dry, then she starts to cough.

"Hang on," I tell her, getting up to pour some water from a pink plastic pitcher on a rollaway tray near the bed. "Here you go. Don't drink too fast."

I hold the straw to her mouth, tipping the cup carefully while she takes a small sip. It's all she can manage; she closes her lips and turns her head away on a winced groan.

"Better?" I ask.

"Not really," she murmurs, her tongue sluggish from the opioids dripping into her veins from the IV. "I'd be better if I wasn't dying."

I nod, knowing there's no need to pretend with Kathryn. She's always been blunt and practical. Fearlessly so.

"Can I get you anything else right now?"

She doesn't answer for a moment, just blinks up at me with bleary, listless eyes. "Is Avery with you?"

"Yes. She stepped outside for a minute." I place the paper cup down on the tray beside the water pitcher. "I'll let her know you're awake."

"Dominic . . . wait. Let me say something to you. Please?"

Lingering in this room is the last thing I want to do, especially now that my mind is swamped with a lot of old memories I thought I'd left behind in Florida. But I figure I owe it to this woman to finally hear her out. Hell, I owe Kathryn Tremont more than I'll ever be able to repay.

A look of mild surprise—and relief—settles over her face when I remain standing at the side of the bed. "Will you always hate me?"

I scowl, realizing just how deeply my anger hurt her. "I never hated you, Kathryn."

"You never loved me, either." She states it matter-of-factly, then closes her eyes. For a long moment, she simply breathes. "Well . . . that's all right. I'm not an easy woman to love."

She motions for me to give her more water. I let her drink, then I use the edge of her sheet to dab at the small trail of liquid that leaks onto her chin.

"You were so young when I saw you that first time," she murmurs, watching me tend her. "Were you even twenty?"

"Just," I reply, recalling the older, beautiful, sophisticated woman who spotted me parking cars at a fancy event not long after I arrived in New York and proceeded to attach me to her arm like one of her flashy baubles. Not that I'd complained. She was mercurial and fascinating to be around. And she had wealth and connections I could never make on my own.

Simply put, we used each other, both of us happy with the arrangement because it served our own selfish goals.

"You had so much to look forward to, Dominic. I sensed that about you from the start. And I only wanted to be the one to help you get there. I wanted to—" Another racking cough seizes her, making her frail body convulse.

I slide my hand to her back, trying to assist her in finding a more comfortable position. Her spine is a knobby ribbon against my palm, her skin cool and clammy beneath her thin hospital gown. When the cough subsides, she takes another small drink then sags against the mattress.

"I never meant to hurt you. That party I arranged in the Hamptons for you—for your art—it was never my intention to embarrass you or make you uncomfortable. I only wanted the rest of the world to see your talent."

"My talent was gone, Kathryn."

I'm shocked to hear the words come out devoid of fury. The regret is still there, but it's not Kathryn who's to blame for what I've lost. It's my father. And me.

I hold up my right hand, the one riddled and ruined with heavy scars. "I was never going to paint again, so parading my work in front of a bunch of people who would only look at me in pity afterward wasn't the kind of help I needed. I sure as hell didn't want it."

"I know," she admits quietly. A sound like a small sob catches in the back of her throat. "I understand that now. And I want you to know I'm sorry that I didn't understand it then."

I shake my head, recalling my self-destructive, unhinged reaction the day of the party when I discovered my art was about to be shown to a room full of critics and media and countless other of Kathryn's society friends. In a blind rage, I savaged it all. Five paintings—the only ones in existence, the only things of value I took with me when I left the old man in my rearview mirror and headed for New York—demolished in a single, stupid act wrought by my own hands.

The irony of it hadn't escaped me, even then.

"Forget it," I tell Kathryn. "That's all ancient history, anyway. It doesn't matter."

"No, Dominic. It does matter. I didn't know what you needed back then." She gazes at me sorrowfully, but without any trace of bitterness. "*I* wasn't what you needed. But that lovely girl outside . . . she is."

My eyes lift, searching for Avery in the corridor. She's listening to Pauline, nodding, her face solemn. My heart constricts at the sight of her, feeling too full for my chest. Yet I can't look away. Everything I want is standing in that hallway. Everything I could ever need.

"Yes," Kathryn says, a note of satisfaction in her drowsy tone. "You know it too. So don't let her down again. Be good to her, Dominic. Be the man she needs."

I want to issue some confident promise that Avery will never need anyone but me. That I can somehow, eventually, prove myself deserving of the honor.

But the words don't come.

I look at Avery and while she grounds me in so many ways, she also holds the power to unravel me. I felt that today, after I nearly ripped open other old scars—ones that can never be sewn shut again once their secrets spill out.

I look at Avery and I feel adrift, in need of her body's soft anchor and the safe port that I haven't found anywhere but in her eyes.

I look at her, miraculously back in my life after I was so certain I'd pushed her away forever, and I am drowning in emotions I never knew before I met her.

I feel utterly out of control with the depth of my love for her.

I reach for a suitably reassuring reply to Kathryn's challenge, but the easy confidence I can usually cloak myself in eludes my grasp. The only thing I find is naked, vulnerable candor.

"I hope I can be what Avery needs."

Kathryn says nothing. I'm not even sure she heard me. When I glance back at the bed, her eyes are closed and her breath is puffing softly through her parted lips.

17

"Okay, Pauline. Thank you for letting me know." I end the call and set my phone down on the cocktail table in Nick's living room.

"Everything okay?"

He walks out from the kitchen barefoot, his white shirt still tucked loosely into his belted suit pants but unbuttoned to his chest and rolled up at the sleeves. Clutched in his hand is a cut-crystal tumbler of whisky. We arrived at the penthouse about an hour ago, our plans for a proper date tonight put on the back burner. With Kathryn hospitalized, the last thing on my mind is going out somewhere. I had planned to go home after the hours spent at Kathryn's bedside, but it didn't take a lot of convincing for Nick to persuade me to stay the night in the city with him in case her situation worsened.

Fortunately, that worry seems to be abated at least for now.

"They're moving her out of ICU tonight. Pauline says the doctors want to observe her for a few hours tomorrow, make sure she's strong enough to go home. There's a good chance Kathryn will be discharged following the afternoon rounds."

"Sounds encouraging."

"I suppose so, all things considered." I fold my legs under me on the sofa. "Pauline thinks it's time for Kathryn to start thinking about hospice."

He doesn't say anything as he takes a seat beside me, just nods then takes a swig from the crystal glass. "You sure I can't fix you a drink?"

"No, thank you." He's on his second since we came home from the hospital, and this one appears to be a larger pour than the first. "Do you want to talk about it?"

He stares at me as if I just said I wanted to discuss my period. "Talk about it?"

"Kathryn's cancer. The fact that she's dying."

"What more is there to say?"

Although he seems accepting enough on the surface, even calm, I study his face as he tips the glass to his lips again and downs another healthy swallow of liquor. There is a storm of dark emotion behind the shuttered control of his gaze. A world of hurt he's holding far out of my reach.

"I know your history with Kathryn, Nick. Are you afraid to tell me that you still care about her?"

He swivels a hard, questioning look at me. "Is that what you think?"

"I don't mean romantically. I know that was over a

long time ago. I mean, are you okay with the way you and she have left things? What I mean is, are there things you need to resolve with her while you still have the time?"

He drains his glass and sets it down on the table. "We've talked." I'm sure my confusion is evident in my face. Nick leans back on the sofa with a sigh, draping his arm behind me. His fingers toy idly in my hair, his touch soothing me while I wait for him to say more. "You were in the hall with Pauline. Kathryn woke up. We spoke for a few minutes. I don't know . . . I guess she felt the need for some kind of absolution from me. Closure, maybe."

"Did you give it to her?"

"I told her there was nothing to forgive. I never hated her, even though I let her believe I did for far too long. She didn't deserve that."

I reach up and stroke his beard-shadowed cheek. "She's been waiting years to hear you say that," I point out gently, well aware of how deeply it hurt Kathryn to feel she'd made an enemy out of him only because she did something motivated by her love for him. I lean into his side, drawn to his warmth, his strength. "Thank you for showing her kindness today, Nick. She needs that kind of peace now more than ever."

His arm comes down around me, tucking me close. "What do you need?"

"You. This." My fingers find their way to the back of his neck and into the silky edge of his black hair. "All I need is us. I see Kathryn so alone at the end of her life and it scares me sometimes."

He frowns, brushing the backs of his fingers along the side of my face. "You're afraid of being alone?"

"No. Afraid of going through my life without you."

"Angel." The word is a rough whisper just before his lips meet mine. His kiss is deep and possessive, flavored with need and the sweet, smoky flavor of the whisky on his tongue.

I didn't come here tonight with the intention of making love, but when Nick is kissing me like this, there's no room for anything else. He makes me feel safe. He makes me feel cherished and protected, as if nothing bad can ever touch me so long as I'm in his arms.

I need to feel those things now—more than I realized.

After being in that hospital around so much talk of sickness and dying, I need to feel alive.

I need to feel secure in Nick's love.

His kiss turns hotter before I'm fully prepared. With his tongue stroking against mine, devouring my soft moans and panting breaths, he pushes me down onto the sofa beneath him. As much as I ache to feel him against me, his need seems even more urgent. He draws back on a groan, then makes quick work of my loose top and denim shorts. His mouth is hungry on me, traveling over every inch of bared skin, his teeth nipping me sharply when he reaches my hip.

"I have to taste you," he growls, already dragging my panties down my legs.

If I craved a slow burn tonight, it's clear that Nick has other ideas.

He spreads me wide, then descends, his dark head buried between my thighs. There is no prelude, and no mercy in the assault he wages on my sex. It's wet and hot and fevered.

There's no slowing him down, but then it's easy to

get caught up in the storm of his intense passions. And seeing him so consumed with lust for me is a pleasure all its own.

I cry out in protest when his mouth leaves me just when my climax was building toward its peak. Straddling me with one foot on the floor and the other knee bent on the side of me, he strips out of his shirt and tosses it aside. His eyes are turbulent with need as he unfastens his belt and draws down the zipper of his bespoke slacks. He pulls his cock out, his hand wrapped around the hard length, stroking it all the way to the plump, glistening head as he moves nearer to my face.

"Take it." His voice is low and demanding. "I need your mouth on me now."

I can't obey him fast enough. Arousal spirals through me, as sharp and compelling as Nick's command. I close my lips around him and suck him deep, moaning at the feel of him on my tongue, filling my mouth. His hands mold to the back of my head as I move up and down on him. He shows me the tempo he wants, the pressure of his fingers urging me to go deeper, faster, harder.

"Fuck," he grinds out tersely as he powers into my mouth.

I know he's on the verge of coming and I want to take him there. I cup his balls and meet every furious stroke, even though it's almost too much for me to manage. On a violent curse, he pulls me off him and shoves me down onto my back. His slacks and boxer briefs bunch low on his thighs but he doesn't seem to notice or care.

Kneeling between my legs, he yanks my hips up to meet him, his scarred hand guiding his cock roughly into the folds of my slick, swollen cleft. He thrusts inside, tunneling deep and hard, as far as my body will allow. It's almost too much. He's immense and tonight he's got the sexual hunger to match. There is an air of domination in him now that unsettles me, even though it once turned me on.

Nick's eyes are locked onto mine but they seem remote, shuttered as he moves inside me. His hips rock urgently, violently, leaving no room for the tenderness I crave. I don't know what's spurring this animal need in him, if it's the alcohol or the hospital or the dark, troubled mood that seemed to ride him most of the day. Maybe it's all of those things.

He doesn't give me any chance to reach him.

Pulling out of me on a harsh snarl, he lifts me under the arms and turns me around, positioning me on my knees and then pressing me down atop the arm of the sofa. With my hands caught in his grasp at my back, he enters me from behind, bucking into me with even greater frenzy. I can't deny the erotic pleasure that streaks through me to be pinned beneath him, submitted completely and wholly at his mercy.

But this isn't what I need right now.

I need to see his face. I need to touch him, and feel his arms around me.

I crave an intimacy I don't think he's capable of tonight.

"Nick," I gasp, struggling to find my breath, let alone the words. "Nick, please . . ."

I don't know if he hears me. He seems too far gone into whatever it is that owns him right now.

And then I hear the soft jangle of a belt buckle. Followed by the fluid whisper of cool leather being wrapped around my wrists at my back.

"Nick . . . no." I flinch, a jolt of alarm shooting into my veins. I tamp it down, knowing he would never hurt me or do anything I don't want. "Not like this, okay? Not tonight."

Nick and I have played at games like this before, but something is different about him tonight. I don't know why he feels the need for this kind of control right now, but he is lost to it. I sense a darkness in him so strongly it startles me. Terrifies me.

And the leather doesn't leave my wrists; it only tightens. Everything inside me freezes in an instant.

"Nick?" I turn my head to look at him over my shoulder but his eyes are wild and vacant. "Dammit, Nick. I said no!"

I scramble away from him. Pulling my hands out of his hold and kicking free of the sofa, I fall to the floor in an inelegant sprawl. I sit up, naked and shaking. My breath heaves in and out of my lungs as I stare up at him in shocked silence.

I'm not sure which of us is more horrified.

"Avery—*fuck*."

He reaches for my hand to help me up, but I don't take it. I move away from the sofa in a rush of limbs then slowly stand up, easily out of his reach.

"Now you're afraid of me?" His face is a mask of contrition . . . and barely contained fury. "Jesus Christ."

He swings his feet to the floor and stands, pulling up his black boxer briefs and pants and tucking his still-erect cock inside. He zips up tersely and reaches for his empty glass on the table.

I swallow hard, searching for words as I watch him stride away from me toward the kitchen. Hastily putting on my clothes, I follow after him.

"What was that about, Nick? What the hell were you doing?"

"I thought it was obvious."

His flippant reply stops me cold in my tracks. I watch from behind him as he pours two fingers of liquor into the glass. I wince as he throws it back in one gulp. "Do you really think more alcohol will help?"

He grunts, not bothering to face me. "It's been known to in the past."

"Oh, really? You mean like the night you almost put a gun to your head in the back office at the gallery?" The glare he swivels on me nearly sends me back a pace. I'm sure that's his intent, but I hold my ground. "Talk to me. Tell me what's bothering you. Does it have something to do with Kathryn's cancer? The fact that she's dying?"

"This has nothing to do with her."

It's not much of answer, but at least he's talking. "Was it the hospital, then? I noticed how uncomfortable you were there."

"For fuck's sake." Forgoing the glass, he grabs the bottle of single malt and stalks past me, back into the living room. "Stop trying to analyze me, Avery. If I wanted a therapist I'd fucking hire one."

"Maybe you should."

He barks out a caustic laugh. Still keeping me at his back, he walks to the large living room window that looks down over Manhattan's nighttime skyline and the two glistening rivers that flank the island. The first night he brought me here, I stood in front of that window marveling at the view below and the darkly handsome, mysterious man who had invited me into his world.

Dominic Baine had been a fascinating puzzle to me, one I couldn't wait to solve.

Now I can't help wondering if I'll ever know him.

Will he ever truly let me in?

"What were you going to say to me earlier today at the rec center, Nick?" I watch his body tense at the question. The change that sweeps over him is almost palpable. "When I said I was proud of you, something happened. Did it have something to do with your past? Maybe something about your father, or the fight the two of you had that injured your hand?"

"Drop it, Avery." He pivots around to face me now, his jaw clamped. Finally, he blows out a short breath. "You're making something out of this that isn't there."

"Am I?" I slowly shake my head. "I don't think so. I don't think the way you're acting with me now is nothing."

"How I'm acting?" He holds his arms out, the web of scars gleaming on his forearm and his right hand, which is wrapped around the neck of the half-empty bottle of whisky. I notice he's not quite steady on his feet. "You said you needed to fuck, so we fucked. Now you're looking for reasons to fight with me."

Anger and hurt surges up inside me like a black wave I can't stop. "I didn't need to fuck tonight. I needed tenderness from you, Nick. I needed comfort. Connection. Things you seemed willing and capable of giving me a few nights ago, so why not now?" I hate the way my voice trembles, the way my whole body shudders with the raw ache of my disappointment. "I told you that if we had any chance of making it, there couldn't be any more lies or secrets—and you agreed. You agreed there would be no more games of control. No more power plays."

"And what if I can't do that?"

I take a step back, almost staggering at his quiet reply.

Now he's the one who advances. He moves toward me, holding me in a penetrating stare that terrifies me as much as it breaks my heart. "What if those are promises I can't keep?"

I swallow hard, a coldness opening up in the middle of my chest. "Then we're only wasting each other's time, Nick."

He doesn't say anything. Not a damn word. I want to scream and rail at him but I don't have the strength to summon anger when I'm still reeling from the body blow of everything he just said.

"I should go," I murmur.

"That's probably for the best." His answer is equally as wooden as I feel.

Oh, God. Is this really happening?

I don't want to believe it.

My hands are shaking as I pivot around to retrieve my shoes. I put them on, collecting my phone and slipping it back into my purse.

"I'll call Patrick," Nick offers from behind me, his tone so reasonable I want to scream. "He'll see you home safely."

I cringe at the idea of his driver being summoned to schlep me back to Queens. "Don't bother. I can get home on my own."

I glance at Nick and find he's already turned away, staring out at the darkness on the other side of the large window.

As I slip out the door and close it behind me, my exit is punctuated by the jarring crash of a bottle hitting a wall.

18

My phone rings for the third time this morning, Nick's number lighting up the screen. Ignoring the pang in my breast, I mute the call and send it straight to voicemail—just as I have all the other times he's tried to reach me in the past couple of days.

He's left messages, but I can't bring myself to listen to them yet. I don't want to hear his excuses or apologies. Even worse, I don't want to hear accusations that I overreacted or that I'm being unreasonable in my demand that we strive for something more than just sheet-scorching sex and amazing orgasms.

I want something real with him.

I want his heart as open to me as mine is to him.

I thought it was, or that we were working toward it

at least. At his penthouse the other night I saw that I was wrong. Evidently what I need are things he's not capable of giving me.

Maybe Nick isn't capable of giving himself to anyone like that.

"Avery?" My mother's voice sounds from somewhere behind me, inside the rustic Pennsylvania lake house that once belonged to my grandparents.

It's early, not even eight o'clock, but I've been up for a while already, soaking up the solitude of this place I used to love as a child. There is a tranquility here, comfort in the memories of being on the lake with my grandpa in his small sailboat, and decorating Christmas cookies with my grandmother when I was a little girl. Years before my daddy, Daniel Ross, died. And long before my mother met Martin Coyle, the monster who became my stepfather.

"Avery, honey? Where are you, baby?"

"Out here, Momma." Seated on one of the old rocking chairs on her back porch, I set my phone facedown on the wicker table next to me and try to erase the sadness from my face.

I've been here at her house for the past two days, having taken a bus out of the city to Scranton where my mother picked me up. It's only been a few weeks since my last visit, but considering we have a decade of separation to make up for since her parole from prison eight months ago, I don't think I'll ever be able to see her enough.

But it's not only that. I needed somewhere soft to fall after my fight with Nick.

I'm not ready to call it a breakup, but right now it's difficult for me to see a clear path toward anything else with him.

The screen door creaks as my mom steps out to join me on the covered porch. "Well, there you are. You're up early again today. How long have you been sitting here, honey?"

I shrug. "For a little while, I guess. I just wanted to watch the lake."

She makes a pleased sound, somewhere between a sigh and a hum. "I spend a lot of time out here too."

Paused where she stands, she simply looks out at the landscape before her. I see her small smile grow as she drinks in the tree-studded, gently sloping hill that leads down to the rickety wooden dock below and the tranquil lake that glistens like quicksilver under the pale morning light. She's wearing a long cotton nightgown with tiny butterflies printed on it. Her feet are bare, and I can't hold back my own smile when I see the bright red polish on her toes, and the sun-kissed color of her tan skin.

Her once-blonde hair has turned yellowish gray and her face is lined beyond her fifty-one years, but she is still beautiful. Still the vibrant, strong woman I admired all my life.

After the decade she spent in a small prison cell convicted of killing my abusive stepfather, she is finally free.

Thanks mostly to Nick.

"I thought maybe we could go to the farmer's market this morning," she says. "We can get a bunch of fruit and some peppers and onions to put on those kabobs we've got marinating for dinner tonight." She turns an eager look on me. "You might even be able to twist my arm into making Grandma's apple dumplings."

My mouth practically waters at the idea alone.

"Brownies last night and dumplings today? You're spoiling me."

"Yes, I am. And I've been waiting a good long time to have the chance, so you're going to let me spoil you however I want to."

"Even if it puts twenty pounds on my hips?"

She laughs, full-throated and joyful. It almost makes me forget about everything that's going wrong in my life back in New York.

Almost.

She walks over to me and leans down, cradling my head against her breast as she kisses the top of my head. "Do you have any idea how much I love you?"

I nod. "Yes, Momma. I love you too."

She's quiet for a while, just holding me close like she used to do when I was a child. "How long do you plan to hide up here at the lake with me?"

I draw back, lifting my gaze to her. "I'm not hiding."

I've told her about Nick—more or less. She knows I love him, and that I spent the past year miserable without him, despite all of my other personal successes. As of last night she also knows it was Nick's money and connections that helped make her parole happen. I figure I owed it to him to give him that credit.

What I haven't explained to her are the darker nuances of my relationship with him. I've glossed over the things that would only make her worry about me or question the soundness of my judgment when it comes to men. But Nick isn't just any man. And I don't expect anyone, perhaps especially my mother, to be able to understand the kind of relationship we have.

Or had.

I blow out a sigh, uncertain how to explain it to

myself after what happened the other night.

She combs her fingers through my hair, sweeping it away from my face. "Is he a good man, sweetheart?"

"Yes." I press my lips flat, shaking my head in frustration over all the good things I know Dominic Baine to be. "He's a very good man, Mom. The problem is he doesn't know that."

"Not your job to fix him, baby." She looks at me solemnly, sagely. "The only one who can do that is him."

I nod because she's right and I know it.

I can't fix what's broken in Nick any more than he can fix what will always be broken in me.

But what hurts even more than failing is the fact that he won't even trust me enough to give me the chance to try.

There's still a hopeful part of me that believes he needs me as much as I need him. He just has to be willing to see that too.

He only has to love me enough to finally let me in.

Fool that I am, I actually thought he might.

I smile up at my mom. She's concerned about me, and I don't want to burden her with my unhappiness. She's already carried enough of my burdens over the years. "Let's get to the market early, okay? And when we get back, we can make those apple dumplings together."

19

"Avery, pass me that icing bowl and scraper, will you, honey?"

"Sure thing." Mom's washing dishes from our baking while I'm working at the chopping board cutting vegetables for our lunch salads. I set down the bright red pepper I'm dicing and reach over to fetch the metal mixing bowl that's sticky with sweet, buttery vanilla sauce.

"Can't let this go to waste," I say, grinning as I swirl the rubbery spatula around the sides of the bowl, then stick the end of it in my mouth.

She laughs and shakes her head, making room for me to step in beside her and put the items in the sink. It's been a good day with her. I didn't realize how badly I needed the kind of slow-paced, easy companionship that she and I have always had together.

With the windows open and a warm afternoon summer breeze blowing in off the lake, carrying the fragrance of warm cinnamon and apples through the entire house, I cling to the simplicity of the moment like the small slice of heaven it truly is.

But it's only close to perfect because part of my heart is three hours away from me in New York.

Maybe she hears my sigh as I go back to my cutting board and resume the rhythmic chopping. Or maybe it's just maternal intuition that makes her too aware of the undercurrent of contemplative gloom that I haven't been able to set aside all day.

She dries her hands, then wraps her arms around me from behind, her chin resting on my shoulder. "If you'd rather go back home to the city tonight instead of staying for dinner, I'll understand, you know."

"What?" I set down my knife and scoop the peppers into a small prep bowl. "I don't want to leave. I'm exactly where I want to be, Mom. I'm where I need to be right now."

"I'm not so sure about that." Releasing me, she moves to my side and leans back against the butcher block island so I have to look at her. "I think what you really need is to talk things out with this young man of yours."

It almost makes me laugh to hear her refer to Dominic Xavier Baine, billionaire corporate titan, as my "young man". She's never met him, and I'm not sure she's fully grasped the magnitude of who he is in the world of global industry and megadeals. To her, Nick is simply the man her daughter has fallen in love with. The man I continue to love even though he keeps breaking my heart open every time I think it's starting to heal.

He hasn't tried to call again since this morning. After my mom and I came back to the lake house, I listened to the messages he left on my phone. I'd been dreading that I'd hear a lot of empty promises and apologies, or arguments that I had overreacted the other night. Instead Nick's messages were brief, succinct.

I miss you.

I love you.

Please call me.

I've started to dial his number more than once, ultimately deciding that whatever we needed to say to each other is too consequential to take place on a phone call.

And if I'm being totally honest with myself, I'm terrified that the next time I talk to him might be the last—that after coming together based on lies and deception, we may never be able to find our way to a place of truth.

My mother sighs, hooking a strand of my loose hair behind my ear as I pick up the knife and start taking out my frustrations on a handful of multi-colored heirloom tomatoes. "Well, you know your own heart, honey. Just know that I'm always going to be here for you."

"I know, Momma." I glance at her and smile. "I love you."

"I love you, too, baby."

She goes back to the sink while I finish up the salad preparation and stow everything in the refrigerator. I've just put away the last bowl of vegetables when the front doorbell rings.

"Oh, that's probably my new neighbor," she says, setting down the pot she's washing. "I let her borrow my weed whacker last week and she keeps promising to bring it back."

Shaking off her wet hands, she reaches for the towel draped through a cabinet pull.

"That's okay, Mom. I'll get the door."

I head through the small house to the screen door out front. My feet stop abruptly, and for a second I just stand there, frozen in place.

It's not Mom's neighbor.

It's Nick standing on the shaded stoop of my grandparents' old house. Despite the heat, he's dressed in jeans and a navy T-shirt that only sets off the bright cerulean color of his eyes. Eyes that are fixed on me with breathtaking intensity from the other side of the flimsy wood-framed screen door.

"Hi," he says.

Just one word. A single syllable that releases an entire wave of emotion inside me.

I swallow, searching for my voice. "What are you doing here?"

I don't mean for it to sound so unwelcome. I see the flicker of doubt in his gaze. I see it in the way he doesn't move at all, standing rigidly in front of me, his hands held down at his sides.

I take a breath and try again. "Isn't the ribbon-cutting ceremony for the recreation center happening today?"

"It was. I postponed it."

I stare at him. "You postponed it . . . to come here?"

"I need to talk to you, Avery. I need—" He breaks off abruptly and rakes his hand over his scalp. "Ah, Christ. I just . . . needed to see you. Everything else can wait."

Even the rec center, the dream he's nurtured from concept to completion.

Could he actually mean that? The fact that he's standing here leaves little room for doubt.

"Nick, you shouldn't have done that. The rec center—"

"It will wait," he insists. "As for things I shouldn't have done, that's a long list. I hoped we could talk about it."

"Avery, is everything okay?" My mom steps beside me, cautious when she realizes it's a man waiting outside.

"Mom, this is Nick."

"Oh. Hello." She scrutinizes him, her arm coming up around me as if to let me know I don't have to face him alone if I'm not ready to.

"Pleasure to meet you, Mrs. Ross." Nick gives her a subtle nod of greeting, and I notice that he chooses to refer to her by my father's last name instead of Coyle, that of the unworthy monster she made the mistake of marrying after Daddy died. "I just drove up from New York. I was hoping I could speak to your daughter for a while."

"It's not me you need to ask." Her frank response makes his mouth quirk in just the barest smile.

"Yes, ma'am," he agrees. He glances back at me and I can see the hope in his eyes. I can see the fear in them too. "Avery, will you let me talk to you? Please."

I reach for the cool metal latch of the screen door. "Let's go for a walk."

We end up at the lake on the wooden dock in back of the house. I'm not surprised my feet guide me there; I often did some of my clearest thinking sitting on the end of the long plank walkway with my toes dangling in the cold, dark water. I do that now, stepping out of my flip-flops and sinking down onto the sun-bleached wood.

Nick follows my lead, toeing off his Gucci loafers and cuffing the legs of his jeans before seating himself next to me. "You look a lot like your mom."

I nod. "Everyone used to say that. She was so much prettier, though. She looked like an angel in the wedding pictures I have of her and my dad."

"I'm sure she did." Nick stares out at the water, a small, private smile curving his lips. "Is this the lake you used to visit with your grandfather?"

"This is it." I mentioned the lake to him only once, sharing with him how I used to enjoy spending time on the water with Grandpa on his little sailboat. It's surreal to be sitting next to Nick on this dock now, even if our reasons for being out here are less than ideal.

"I can see why this place is special to you. It's so peaceful out here."

I sigh, looking out over the glistening ripples that spread out before us. "No matter how hard things got for Mom and me, when we'd come out here to the lake it seemed like nothing bad could touch us. I never felt safer than when I was right here on my grandparents' dock."

"That's something I never had growing up."

His quiet admission draws my gaze to him. "You weren't close with your grandparents?"

"No."

"Why not?"

He shrugs, staring straight ahead yet at nothing in particular. "My mom's parents were from up north. They had money, from what I understand. They didn't approve of her marriage to my dad, but she was already pregnant with me so there wasn't much they could say about it. Mom told me they cut her off soon after she informed them I was on the way."

"What an awful thing for them to do. I'm sorry, Nick."

"No loss, since I never met them. Never even saw their faces."

He says it nonchalantly, but I can't imagine what it's like for a child trying to understand why his own blood would want nothing to do with him sight unseen. "And what about your dad? Did you at least know his parents?"

It takes him a moment to answer, as if he's searching for the right words. "When I was still a baby, my grandmother put a shotgun under her chin and pulled the trigger. As for my old man's father, he was a violent drunk so I did my best to steer clear of the bastard."

I close my eyes, trying to hold back my horror at the grim picture he's painted. I didn't mean for our conversation to stray into this awful territory, but it's the first time Nick has ever opened up to me about the people in his early life or the way he grew up.

"But you did have the water," I remind him gently.

When Nick took me to Miami last year and we spent several days aboard his beautiful sailboat, *Icarus*, he told me that he practically grew up on the ocean. Now I wonder if the water was more of an escape to him than a safe harbor like it had been for me.

"I sailed to get away from the life I had on land," he says, confirming my suspicions. "My father was a fisherman. So was his father before him. All the Baine men for several generations made their living off the swamps and inlets of the Keys."

"But not you?"

"Not me. The old man wouldn't even teach me how to hold a fishing rod." He laughs humorlessly. "He pretty much hated me from the day I was born."

I wince to hear it, my heart refusing to believe Nick could be right. "Why would you think that?"

"He made it clear enough, believe me. He disapproved of everything I did. Ridiculed me constantly about being too weak, too useless to go out on the boat with him. Called me a sissy because I liked to draw and paint like my mother. Fortunately, he wasn't home much. When most of the good fishing dried up he opened a swamp boat charter and made his living off tourists."

"Your father couldn't have been more wrong about you, Nick. You're the strongest man I know—in every way that matters. There's nothing useless about you."

He gives me a faint, wry smile. "I guess I should thank the bastard for driving me to make something of myself. Baine International is the ultimate fuck you to that sadistic son of a bitch."

I reach up and stroke the back of his head. It's the first time I've touched him since he's been here, and while I'm not sure we'll find our way back to the place our relationship needs to be, right now I want Nick to know that I care. That I believe in him and always will.

And as much as it hurts me to hear about his father's unconscionable treatment of him, I can't help but latch on to the one ray of light amid all of the bleakness he's described. "Your mom . . . she was an artist too?"

"Not professionally. She gave that dream up when she married my old man. But yes, she was incredibly gifted."

"You've never mentioned her before."

"No."

"Why not, Nick?" I'm terrified that he's going to tell me that she treated him hideously too. But I have to know. "Was she as cruel as your father?"

"God, no. She was as kind as she was beautiful and gifted. She was the only good thing I had in my life."

My relief leaks out of me on a deep exhalation. "Then I don't understand. How could she allow your father to treat you that way?"

"She didn't know how bad it was. I didn't want her to think I was weak and useless too." He glances away from me again, his gaze retreating back to the large expanse of the lake. "And then, when I was ten years old she got cancer. The doctors said she could beat it, but nothing worked. None of the painful chemo treatments. None of the medicines that made her vomit and writhe as if her insides were being ripped out." He exhales heavily, then hisses a low curse. "I sat at her bedside every day for seven months, the last few spent at the hospital. I watched her die in agony, felt her slipping away a breath at a time those last few weeks."

"Oh, Nick." I take his hand in mine. The raised spider webs of scars are smooth beneath my touch as I gently rub my thumb over the back of his hand. "That's why you've seemed so uncomfortable around Kathryn at her house. And at the hospital. I'm sorry if all of that brought back uncomfortable memories."

He lifts his shoulder. "I haven't stepped foot in a hospital since my mother died—other than the emergency room I was ambulanced into the night my father sent me through that window eight years later."

"Where is your father now?"

He slants me a sardonic look. "We haven't kept in touch."

"Is he still alive?"

"I wouldn't give a damn either way."

He shakes his head, going somewhere distant now in his mind. I can see the way his gaze detaches from me. He's sitting beside me, but I feel him starting to drift out of my reach again.

I have to wonder how much of the unreachable, tormented man I saw the other night was shaped by everything Nick went through as a child.

A truly awful thought begins to take shape in my mind as I look at him and process all he's said about the violence and degradation he suffered at his father's hands.

What if the abuse went further than mental and physical? My stomach roils at the idea because I've been there too. Without my mother to protect me, I doubt I would have survived.

And from what he has just described, he had no one after his mother died. Not a single person in his family whom he could turn to.

"Nick, that night you fought with your father eight years ago . . . how did it start?"

He shrugs, too quickly, I think. "I don't remember. We were both drunk. Started saying things neither one of us wanted to hear."

I recall the few details he's told me about the confrontation that almost cost him his right hand if not half his arm. Whatever words were said were volatile enough for his father to nearly kill Nick in his rage.

"You told me once that your father knocked you

through that window because he wanted to shut you up," I remind him quietly. "What was it that he didn't want to hear?"

"I don't know. Something stupid, probably." Nick draws his hand out of my loose grasp. He takes in a long breath, then lets it gust out of him sharply. "I don't remember much about that night. It's not important anymore."

He's lying to me. I accept it without feeling stung, but I am troubled by what telling this lie is doing to him. I can feel the edge of desperation in it. He's keeping a secret and it's eating him alive.

A chill sweeps over me because I'm terrified that I know what it is. I've survived something equally abhorrent too.

I don't want to push him to say words he's not ready to speak, but I can't let him think he's alone anymore. I need him to understand that I'm someone he can turn to now. I always will be.

"Nick, did your father ever . . ."

On a curse, he swings a wild, repulsed look on me. "No. Never. Jesus Christ, he was an asshole but he never touched me. Not like that."

Thank God. My chest feels tight and I realize I'd been holding my breath waiting for his answer. I look for some hint that he's not being truthful, but all I see in his face is outrage that I would even think such a thing.

Maybe my sense was wrong about the nature of his abuse by his father, but I'm still not convinced that he doesn't remember every detail about the night he and his father nearly killed each other.

"I'm sorry, Nick. I just . . . I had to ask."

"I know." His expression relaxes into something

tender, all of his attention focused on me. He cups my face in his palms. "Every time I think of what your stepfather did to you, Avery, I wish I had been the one to end him. I would've made him suffer a hell of a lot more than you or your mother did."

I nod, knowing he means it. "What happened to me is over. I came through it. My mom came through it too. A lot of the reason I can say that now is you, Nick."

"Even after the other night?" He brushes the pad of his thumb across my lips. "I don't have any excuses, Avery. You said no and that should've been enough."

"You told me once that I'd never need a safe word with you."

"And you don't. You won't, not ever again." His curse is soft but vivid. "What I did was wrong. I failed you. Christ, I scared you."

I shake my head. "I wasn't afraid. I was disappointed."

His gaze drops to my mouth as if he wants to kiss me but won't permit himself to do anything more than simply hold on to me. "I hate that I lost control the way I did. With the alcohol and with you."

"It seemed to me that you needed that control. And I don't think it had anything to do with the whisky you were drinking."

He absorbs my words for a long moment, so long I'm not even sure he's going to respond. When he does, his deep voice has a tremor to it, as if his emotions are almost too much for him to contain. "Do you have any idea how much I love you, Avery? I've never felt this close to a woman before—not to anyone. I need you. I can't function when you're not with me. And that scares the living fuck out of me."

He draws me closer, holding my face as if I'm made of glass yet looking at me with a raw ferocity that shocks me. All the things he says he feels, I feel for him too.

"After Paris, I felt what it was like to lose you, Avery. Now that you're here with me again, I'm scared to fucking death that you're going to slip away from me."

My smile wavers on my lips. "So instead you push me away like you did the other night?"

"I'm sorry." He strokes my cheek, then tunnels one hand into my hair, his palm at my nape. "I'm so sorry for the way I treated you, the things I said. I didn't mean them. I can't offer excuses. I can only promise you that it will never happen again."

I close my eyes, wanting to believe him. Needing to believe he can keep that promise.

"All the things you said you needed from me," he whispers fiercely. "Those are the things I want too. I just don't know how to ask for them. I'm not sure I know how to give them. But I want to try."

"I have to see those words in action, Nick." I swallow past the thickness in my throat. "Giving you that chance might require more trust than I have to give you right now."

He nods solemnly. "What can I do to prove it to you?"

"This is a start. You coming here was a start."

A look of relief fills his handsome face. "After you ignored all of my calls, I wasn't sure you'd be willing to listen."

"And you came anyway?"

"There isn't anywhere else I want to be." He caresses my cheek, a barely restrained yearning in his brilliant blue eyes. "Would it be all right if I kissed you now, Ms.

Ross?"

My heart is so full and hopeful, I can't hold back my smile. "I'll be disappointed if you don't, Mr. Baine."

20

After staying for dinner and apple dumplings with me and my mom, Nick spent the night on the worn-out plaid sofa in the living room.

It's too soon to know if our talk will be the lasting balm our relationship needed, but in the three days since we've been back in the city, Nick and I have been practically inseparable. True to his word, he's giving me all that I asked of him—more, in fact.

I've never felt so cherished, so adored. He's been tender and attentive every hour we're together, careful to give me no reason to doubt him. Making love he's been infinitely patient, allowing me to set our pace, even when the heat between us is at its hottest. Even when I can tell how much it's costing him to surrender the control he has so often wielded as a weapon—and a shield.

"Hey, beautiful." His deep voice is like a warm caress as he strolls into the penthouse bathroom, where I've just come out of the shower. The sight of him shirtless in just a pair of well-worn faded jeans makes my stomach flip. "I've been in the study on the phone with Beck. Have you been home long?"

Home. I can't contain the smile that curves my lips upon hearing him say that. Even though I don't have plans to move out of my own house, nor has he asked me to, Nick's place does feel like home. Being here with him is easy, the most natural thing in the world, and for a moment I simply allow myself to savor the feeling.

"I got back from Kathryn's a few minutes ago," I tell him, meeting his smile in the vanity mirror in front of where I sit. I'm wearing a silk robe, my hair wrapped up in a white towel. "What time will Patrick be driving us to the recreation center?"

"Four-thirty. The ribbon-cutting isn't until six, but there will be press photos and interviews to deal with beforehand." He walks up behind me and rests his palms on my shoulders, leaning down to kiss the side of my neck. "You smell delicious."

So does he. I close my eyes and breathe in that unique mix of warm, clean skin and masculine spice that's been stamped indelibly into my senses from the moment I first brushed up close to him. If we had more than an hour before we're due to leave for the rec center that scent and the press of his mouth below my ear might tempt me right back into bed with him.

It still might.

He withdraws much too soon for my liking. His hands linger on me, though, caressing me lightly as his gaze holds mine in the glass. "How was Kathryn feeling today?"

"The same. She slept a bit more today than yesterday when I stopped by to see her."

"Has there been any more talk about hospice?"

I press my lips together, shaking my head. "Pauline says Kathryn refuses to acknowledge the possibility. Each time I tried to bring up the subject with her, she deflected."

Nick grunts. "It's not like her to avoid an uncomfortable issue. She's always preferred to tackle them head-on." He strokes the side of my face. "Like someone else I know."

I pivot in the velvet upholstered vanity chair and look up at him. "She didn't seem to have the energy to talk much today. All she wanted to do is have me tell her about my art, what I'm working on now and when my next showing will be. She even made me write it on her calendar so she could make sure to be there."

"Mind over matter," Nick suggests gently, leaning his hip against the marble countertop. "Maybe making plans helps her feel more in control of the time she has left."

"Maybe. Tomorrow morning she's leaving for a couple of weeks at her house in the Hamptons. When we said goodbye today, she just held me for the longest time."

The look he gives me is filled with solemn consideration. "If you'd rather skip the ribbon-cutting so you can spend more time with her today, I'll understand."

"No. I want to be with you." I take his hand and press a kiss to his palm. "Today is a big deal, Nick.

Besides, Kathryn would never allow me to miss the ceremony. She knows the rec center is also important to me."

He nods, cupping my face. His glance strays to the vanity counter, where I've laid a few pieces of jewelry I plan to wear today. One of those pieces is a diamond encrusted gold-and-platinum watch. One that carries a price tag I could never afford, not even now.

A look of mild surprise—and pleasure—lights the gaze that swings back to me. "You still have the watch I gave you in Paris."

"I still have it."

The stunning Cartier watch was on my wrist the day I left Nick's flat, devastated after learning how he'd orchestrated our meeting in the beginning and perpetuated the lie for the entire time we'd been together. It was the only thing I took from him when I left Paris, and only because I didn't realize the expensive gift was still clamped around my wrist until I was standing in the security line at the airport on my way back to the States.

"I haven't worn it since Paris. I couldn't."

He nods as if he already knew that. Of course, he knows. He understands me better than anyone.

"You were going to wear it for me today?"

"Yes."

He picks it up, silent as he contemplates the jewels that glitter on the watch's face. Then he carefully places it on my wrist the same way he did that morning on the rooftop terrace of his flat.

"I wanted Paris to be our new start," he says as he fastens the delicate clasp. He slowly shakes his head. "I wasn't ready then. I wanted to reset the clock, but I wasn't prepared to be the man you need. I knew I couldn't be the man you deserve, Avery. I'm not sure I'll ever be what you deserve."

"That's not something you can decide, Nick." I ease my arm out of his grasp and get up from the chair. "What I deserve is up to me to decide. But I know what I want. There's only one man I need, and I'm looking at him."

"Avery." He utters my name on a quiet breath and draws me into his arms. His kiss is tender but deep, his tongue licking into my mouth even though I can feel the barely restrained hunger that vibrates through his powerful body.

"I love you," he murmurs against my lips. "Fuck, Avery. Don't ever leave me again."

I close my eyes as the harshly whispered demand skates hotly against my cheek.

He asking for a promise I can't fully give, not when my conscience warns that he and I still have bridges left to cross. I've felt it since we spoke at the lake house—a nagging in my gut that as courageously as he shared the bitter details of his past, there are doors he may never allow me to open.

Cradling his firm jaw in my hands, I look into his haunted gaze. "I never want to leave you, Nick. I love you. I need you. I always will."

On a rough, jagged sound, he hugs me close, burying his head into my breast. For the longest time, he doesn't move. Then, abruptly, he releases me.

Pivoting without explanation, he leaves me standing in the bathroom alone, confused.

And a little bit wary when he returns a moment later holding something behind his back.

"There's one more thing I want you to wear for me today." Brilliant blue eyes hold me in an uncertain stare. "Close your eyes."

My breath catches because we've played this game before. Always with him in control, making the demands. Me in total submission.

I can't go down this road with him again. Not the way we have in the past. Our talk out at the lake should have made that clear.

But I close my eyes anyway, because I have to know.

Something cool and sleek comes down around my head, settling around my neck and plunging down between my breasts.

Pearls.

I look down at the long strand that glistens in the soft light. It's not the first time I've worn these. Usually when Nick placed them on me, he did it to restrain me. To make me submit to whatever dark pleasures he had in mind for me. Not that I complained. Sex with Nick was never boring, and even at his most dominant, his focus was always on me.

Until the other night.

"I've been keeping them for you, Avery. I've been waiting for the chance to see you in them again."

He touches the pearls that dip low into my cleavage, his fingers skimming lightly over the gems before feathering across my skin. I can't suppress my shiver of awareness, nor the coil of hot need that stirs to life inside me.

"When I gave these to you the first time, it was to show you that you could trust me. But it was a selfish gift. I gave it to you to please myself." Lifting my chin on the edge of his fingertips, he lifts my eyes to his. "I'm giving them to you now to show you that you can still trust me."

The vulnerability written on his handsome face is too much for me to bear. He's trying to give me everything. Telling me he'll surrender all that he is—all the things that I love about him.

"Nick, I do trust you."

He shakes his head as if he isn't hearing me. "I'm never going to do anything to hurt you. I'd sooner eat a fucking bullet than make you fear me—"

"No." I frame his head in my hands, bringing his brow down to meet mine. I stare into his eyes, needing him to see me. I want him to understand I'm not afraid of the man I see in front of me now. "Nick, I know you won't hurt me. And I'm not afraid of you."

A miserable look washes over him. "The other night—"

"The other night is behind us. Look at me. Feel me." I slip his hand beneath the loose silk of my robe, settling his palm on my breast before guiding him down to my sex. His fingers flex as they meet the slickness of my cleft. "Does that feel like fear? I'm not afraid of you. And I'm not glass that's going to break if you touch me."

I kiss him, pouring all of my desire and need for him into the fevered joining of our mouths. His arms close around me, his hands sliding down to rest on the curve of my ass. I step back, unfastening the tie at my waist.

My thin robe falls away, leaving me naked except for Nick's watch and the long strand of pearls.

His gaze flares with arousal as he looks at me. "Ah, Christ."

I move farther back, until the vanity counter comes up against the backs of my legs. I hop onto it and take hold of the front waistband of Nick's jeans. His erection bulges against the zipper. I free him, lifting the thick shaft and heavy balls in my hand and then pushing his pants and boxer briefs down onto his muscled thighs.

Leaning back onto the cool marble surface, I spread myself open to him, holding his hungered gaze.

The growl that escapes him is animal and wild. It races through me like a lick of flame to the gasoline of my desire. My sex throbs, aching for the full measure of his lust.

"Fuck me," I beg him. "I need you to fuck me now."

He steps close, raw heat radiating off his powerful frame. One hand clamps onto my hip; the other guides the dripping head of his cock to the ready sheath of my body.

He leans into me, taking my mouth in a savage kiss as he penetrates me. The long, hard thrust stretches me, tunneling deep and wrenching a jagged cry from my lips.

"Mmm," I moan as he fills me again. "God, yes. Fuck me, Nick. I need you to fuck me hard."

His answer is a strangled snarl against my ear. "I thought you were never going to ask."

21

Enjoy the rest of your evening, Mr. Baine," the restaurant doorman tells me as I slide into the back of my private limousine behind Avery.

At nine o'clock it's early to be calling it a night, but after spending several hours at the opening ceremony of the recreation center and all of the press hoopla that entailed, I craved a quiet meal with Avery somewhere far away from chattering crowds and flashing cameras. The little hole-in-the-wall, cash-only Italian place in the East Village isn't much to look at, but the home-style cooking has been bringing people back for more than a hundred years.

"That. Was. Amazing," she says once we settle into the car and Patrick pulls away from the curb. "Hands-down the best spaghetti and meatballs I've ever had.

And the chocolate cannoli was insane!"

I smile and take her hand in mine. "I remember you enjoy authentic Italian food, so I thought you might like this place."

"I loved it." She cuddles against me on the wide leather seat. "Today has been incredible."

"I'm glad you were with me at the ceremony," I tell her, draping my arm around her and smoothing my fingers over the soft skin of her arm. "I wouldn't have wanted to share the day with anyone else."

"I wouldn't have missed for anything, Nick. Watching you up there in front of the press and hundreds of kids and their parents, telling them about your vision for the center and what you hope it brings to the community is something I'll never forget."

And I'll never forget looking into the crowd and seeing her there in the front row, her face full of encouragement and excitement . . . and pride. For me. Even after everything I put her through a year ago.

Especially after the things I've done more recently than that.

It's going to take me a while to purge my shame for my behavior the night we came back from the hospital together. That she's agreed to give me another chance is nothing short of a miracle, but then, that's what Avery has been for me from the start.

A miracle I never expected.

The angel I'll do anything to deserve.

She shifts beside me, scooting up and pivoting to face me. "The name you gave the arts center in the building tonight—I didn't realize you were going to dedicate it after your mom."

I nod. "The Elizabeth Xavier Center."

"It's such a fitting tribute to her, Nick. The entire recreation center is really something special. Can you believe all of the creative classes are completely booked up already?"

I blow out a sigh, running a hand over my jaw. "I wasn't expecting that, no."

"That just speaks to the need you're filling in the community. Maybe you should consider expanding."

I chuckle because her mind evidently works similarly to mine. "I texted Lily before we left for the restaurant to schedule a staff meeting to discuss using this center as a model for other areas of the city."

"Why stop there? Every city in the country could use a gathering place like the one you've created. Take your concept national."

I stare at her, struck silent by the depth of my feelings for this woman. I have the faith of corporate giants and people worth many hundreds of millions of dollars, but the belief I see in Avery's face is the one that renders me speechless. It reaches into me, to a place only she has been able to touch.

Christ, her belief in me goes beyond humbling. It staggers me.

It also gives me a strength unlike anything else before in my life.

She makes me believe I can do anything. Be anything.

Overcome anything.

"It's been my dream all along to make this work in a big community and then one day take it wider. I don't mean for money or recognition. I've got enough of one and couldn't care less about the other. I want to do it for the kids who need a place like that. For the ones who don't have anywhere else to go."

"Kids like you," she says quietly, tenderly.

"Yeah. For kids like me."

Her fingers find my hand, the one riddled with ugly scars. Her touch is light, her fingertips following the ghosts of the jagged lacerations.

Usually when I look at my scars—when I so much as think of them—my head fills with all the memories of that night, and the horrors that preceded it. My father's raging voice, the accusations that exploded out of me, all them finally too immense for me to carry any longer. His vicious denials.

His utter repudiation of me, his son.

"You're a good man, Dominic Baine."

"No. I'm not. But I want to be. For you."

"You're the only man I want. The only one I love."

She draws me to her mouth and kisses me. It's unhurried and sweet, yet I can taste the need in it too.

When she draws back, her eyes are heavy-lidded and dusky in the dim glow of the limousine interior and the blur of city lights that streak by on the other side of the windows.

"So, on a proper date scale of one to ten, how am I doing?"

She laughs softly, happiness beaming in her face. "Off the charts."

I grunt in acknowledgment. "If you're referring to this afternoon before we left for the ribbon-cutting, I agree."

Her grin flashes. "Well, it was definitely a good start."

"Are you suggesting you're not finished with me, Ms. Ross?"

"Oh, I'm more than suggesting."

"Is that right?" My brows rise, along with another part of my anatomy that's already gotten a good head start. I glance up at the rearview mirror where my longtime driver's eyes remain dutifully focused on the evening traffic. "Patrick, how fast can you get us to the Park Place building?"

He chuckles. "I'll do my best, sir."

Avery sits up, tilting her face to whisper in my ear. "Who said anything about waiting until we get home?"

She moves my hand onto her thigh, where her skirt rides up just enough for me to skim my fingers into the heat between her legs. Her skin is infinitely soft, burning beneath my fingertips as I slide higher, into the juncture of her thighs.

She's not wearing panties.

Holy fuck.

A shallow gasp races from between her lips when I stroke into the wetness of her bare pussy. My blood pounds, all of it rushing south to my suddenly unbearable erection.

It's not as if I haven't been thinking about being inside her all damn day.

She's wearing a short-sleeved navy dress that somehow manages to look classic and sophisticated while hugging every luscious curve and plunging low enough to showcase the long rope of pearls around her neck.

She caught the eye of every man in viewing distance of her, but her attention never wavered from me. And each moment she spent beside me I felt my chest swell with pride and wonder that this extraordinary, enticing woman is mine.

Now I need to hear her say the words. I need to hear her say them in a pleasured cry of release that leaves no room for doubt.

My free hand hits the privacy screen button without a word of excuse to Patrick.

As soon as we're sealed off from my driver, Avery attacks my mouth in a searing kiss. We should be sated after the way we came together before leaving for the ceremony this afternoon. But that hard, bone-melting fuck was only a prelude to the desire that erupts between us now.

And thank God for that.

It's been torture trying to downshift and take things slow with her the past few nights. I never want to see fear in her face when she looks at me.

I'll never cross that line with her again—that much I can promise her.

But my need for her is immense.

Today she let me know in no uncertain terms that she wants this too.

Hell, on the bathroom countertop today when she spread herself open to me like an offering laid out on the altar, she demanded no less than everything I had to give her.

Hunger rakes me just to recall it. I see that same erotic invitation in her desire-drenched gaze now.

She inches toward the center of the leather seat, her skirt riding high above her naked hips. The string of pearls rolls with the subtle motion of the vehicle. The long strand dips low, creamy baubles sliding against the shadowed cleft of her sex.

"Christ." The curse wrenches out of me, dark and urgent. "You are so fucking beautiful."

Her sensual mouth curves at my praise. With her eyes locked on mine, she reaches down, her fingers moving the pearls in a slow caress between her slick folds. She arches beneath her own hand, her teeth sinking into her bottom lip as a soft moan curls up from the back of her throat.

It's more than I can bear. I descend on her, pushing her thighs wider as my face meets her pussy and I lick into her sweetness. She sucks in a gasp, bucking against me as I tongue her clit.

The pearls are warm and sleek against my face, rolling between us with each hungry movement of my head between her legs. I slide my hands beneath her and angle her so that she is completely at my mercy.

"Oh God," she whispers, her spine undulating in time with my tongue's lashing.

On a low whimper, she rises up to watch me devour her, unabashed in her enjoyment. Her fingers tunnel into my hair at the back of my head, clutching me against her in fevered demand.

"Fuck," she gasps as I hold her darkened gaze and continue my onslaught. "Nick . . . oh fuck."

Small tremors vibrate in the pearls that brush against my mouth as her climax starts to build. When I catch the end of the strand with my tongue and roll it over the hardened bud of her clit, her body shudders, trembling in my hands.

I don't stop until she's coming, until her soft, shallow panting becomes a moan and then a cry of uncontainable pleasure.

Only then do I stop long enough to unfasten my belt and zipper enough to take my stiff cock in my hand and guide it to her. I drive in deep, too lost to be gentle.

Too consumed with love and desire for this amazing woman to exercise any degree of control.

Her arms wrap around me as I stroke into her tightness, her pussy gripping me like a wet, hot fist.

"You're mine," I utter against her mouth.

I hear the plea in my gruff voice and I know she must too. She must feel it in every hammering thrust that takes me to the very limit of what her small, impossibly snug body can accommodate.

And still I can't get deep enough. I never will, not with her.

"Mine, Avery."

"Yours," she says, clutching me as I move inside her. Her beautiful face is slack with pleasure, lips parted on a gasp. "God, Nick, yes . . . only yours."

She starts coming again and her sharp cries spur me into a desperate rhythm. I plunge hard, furious in my need for release now.

My orgasm erupts in a violent rush, flooding her in hot unrelenting bursts. On a coarse snarl, I lower my head to the curve at the base of her neck and shoulder, my teeth taking hold of her soft sinewy flesh as her sheath milks me. Those tiny contractions strip me of all control. I shudder and jerk atop her, wrung out and utterly owned.

God help me, I'll never get enough of this—of her.

"Mine," I whisper harshly.

I don't care if she knows how badly I need to believe that. I need her to understand it too.

My past has stolen so much from me. The other night it almost took her away too.

Never again.

No matter what I have to do to ensure that.

Even if it means I have to walk through hell itself to keep her.

22

I wake up alone in Nick's bed sometime in the middle of the night.

We'd made love again after returning home to the penthouse, then fallen asleep sated and content in each other's arms. My body is still warm, my senses still thrumming from all of the ways we pleasured each other, so it is a jolt to open my eyes and realize he's gone.

The sheets on his side of the big bed are cold. His phone rests on the nightstand where he set it when we went to bed. The room is dark and silent. No light in the adjacent bathroom, nor in the hallway off the large bedroom suite either.

An unreasonable panic sweeps through me when I see no sign of him here at all.

"Nick?" My voice sounds hollow in the darkened,

vacant room.

Apprehension makes my nape clammy as I slip out of bed and set my bare feet down on the rug. Shrugging into the short kimono draped on the small cushioned bench at the end of the bed, I head out of the bedroom and into the living area of the penthouse. He's not there. When I don't find him in the kitchen either, I pad anxiously down the corridor that leads to his office and study.

"Nick? Are you here?"

Next I check the second floor of the palatial eight-thousand square-foot penthouse, worry mounting when I find no trace of him in the library or the entertainment room. He's not in any of the places he might have gone to burn off sleepless hours.

He's not out on one his late-night jogs either. His running shoes are all arranged neatly in the foyer coat closet, not a single pair out of place.

And anyway it's not like him to leave me in the middle of the night without a word.

I think about how troubled he's gotten since we were apart. He's always had his personal demons but he seemed able to keep them at bay until recently. Or had he?

I think back to the private room in the back of Dominion. The wreckage Nick had hidden from me the entire time we'd been together last year. The admission that he'd been walking a razor's edge of despair and torment in the months before we first met.

A dark possibility leaches into my subconscious—one that chills me to so much as consider.

No.

Oh God, no.

"Nick!"

I race back into the bedroom, my mind spinning with a hundred ugly scenarios, each of them with an outcome I'm too terrified to imagine. My heart is in my throat, my pulse hammering so loudly in my temples I almost don't hear the muffled keening sound coming from somewhere nearby. But then I hear it again and I freeze, all my faculties trained on that pitiful, wounded animal noise.

"Nick?" Every cell in my body feels stretched to the point of shattering as I pad in the direction the awful noise seems to come from.

Nick's enormous walk-in closet is open, but dark as pitch inside.

Not so dark that I don't see the large naked shape huddled on the floor in the far corner.

Oh, Nick.

I don't speak now. As soon as I step inside, I recognize instantly that he's not aware of me or even his surroundings. Hunched like a child with his knees bent and his arms banded tightly around them, he rocks back and forth, his eyes open but unseeing. Dreaming even though he appears to be wide awake.

I bite back the soft cry that bubbles up from my throat upon seeing him like this. Naked. Terrified. Caught in a psychic anguish that was strong enough to wrench him from our bed and drive him here into the dark.

I don't know what to do. Part of me knows that waking him might only cause greater pain and fear, yet I can't look away. I can't let him suffer like this alone.

I step closer to him, easing down at his side on the floor. Tentatively, I reach to him, my fingers lighting in his hair, my touch careful, meant only to soothe not startle. Sweat soaks the thick black waves. His big body shivers against me, seeming to tremble all the way to the bone.

When he doesn't flinch away from my caress I wrap my arm around his broad shoulders. He sags into me, his breathing shallow and rapid. The moan I heard him make before starts building once more.

"Shh. It's okay." Holding him against my breast with one arm, I use my other hand to cradle his head, stroking the damp strands of his hair. "You're safe with me, Nick."

"No." The denial is sharp, but whispered low under his breath. He swallows, his head shaking back and forth beneath my hand. "He can hear me. He'll find me in here."

Ice forms behind my sternum—along with a rage unlike I've ever felt before. "Who'll hear you, Nick?" I ask him gently. "Who's going to find you?"

He shakes his head again. "Be quiet. I have to hide or he's gonna find me. He's gonna hurt me again."

Oh, God. I stroke his bulky shoulder, my arms barely long enough to embrace him fully. Yet I understand it's not Nick the man I'm protecting now, it's the boy he once was. The innocent, artistic boy whose father mistreated and maligned for as long as Nick can remember.

And now the sick suspicion I've had about his past—about the abuse he suffered in his childhood—galvanizes into a chilling certainty. Bile climbs up the back of my throat and it takes everything I have not to lose it and start crying. I have be strong for him now. I have to be strong for the child who's still broken and anguished inside.

"No one can hurt you anymore," I whisper, gathering his big body as close as I can against me. "Nothing bad is ever going to find you while we're together."

I don't know if he hears me. I'm not sure I want him to know what I've just witnessed here. I just want him to feel safe.

I think on some level he must. A ragged sigh rasps out of him as he buries his face in my breast.

His grasp on me is unbreakable, as if he is drowning and I am his only life line.

Long minutes pass before his breathing deepens and levels out to something close to normal. It's even longer before the shudders finally begin to subside. I don't know how long we sit like that, huddled together on the floor in the dark.

I only know I'll hold him for as long as it takes.

If he'll let me, I'll hold on to him forever.

23

Somewhere nearby a cell phone rings. I open my eyes at the same time I feel movement behind me and hear Nick's drowsy groan.

It's morning. And we're in bed together, me lying on my side and him spooning me from behind.

The phone's ringer is abruptly silenced, then his arm comes down around my torso and draws me farther into the warmth of his naked body.

His voice croons against my ear. "Good morning."

"What—" I swallow on a parched throat, confusion tangling my thoughts. How did we get here? Had I been dreaming last night?

But no, the lingering queasy feeling in my stomach wasn't put there because of any dream, not even a nightmare.

Nick's anguish a few hours ago—the night terror that pulled him away from me—was real.

As real as his heated body pressing against my naked curves now. The rigid length of his arousal moves in a slow rhythm between my legs, priming me for his entry.

"Nick, last night—"

He kisses my nape, the heat of his mouth on my sensitive skin short-circuiting my already sluggish morning brain. I take a breath and try again.

"How did we get back to bed last night?"

"I carried you." Another kiss, accompanied by the fluid motion of his hips behind me, his cock gliding distractingly through my slick folds. "I'm sorry if I disturbed your sleep."

Disturbed my sleep? I shift on the mattress, extricating myself from the enticing tangle of our bodies. As much as I enjoy the feel of his nakedness against mine, I can't pretend what I witnessed last night didn't actually happen.

Which is apparently what Nick intends to do.

"Nick, we should talk about it." I sigh when the head of his cock seats at the opening of my sex and gently pushes inside. Oh, God. It feels so good. I moan, trying to hold on to my sense of reason but he's not making it easy.

"Stay, baby." His voice vibrates against me while he begins to move in a soothing, seductive rhythm. "I don't want to talk right now, all right? I just want to be inside you like this for a while."

I relax, loving the feel of him. Loving the feel of us.

He groans, and he sounds so content it's hard for me to deny him. Or myself. After the terrifying experience I had with him last night, I need this contentment too. I need this peaceful sense of intimacy, possibly as much as he does.

But I can't give in to it without knowing that he's okay.

I need to understand what he's struggling against because ultimately I am struggling against it now too.

I turn my head and place a tender kiss to the muscled biceps that holds me so tenderly. I know Nick feels me go still in his arms. He slows at my resistance, then stops.

"Am I hurting you?"

His concern wrenches me. "No. But I'm hurting for you, Nick."

I move out of the circle of his embrace, closing my eyes in regret as our bodies separate. Rolling to face him, I place my hand against the beard-roughened shadow that darkens his cheek. His eyes search mine, yet I can see how badly he wants to hide from me right now.

"I'm worried about what happened last night," I confess gently. "I'm worried about what I saw."

His lips flatten with the furrowing of his brow. "I sleepwalk sometimes. Just a bad habit that comes and goes sometimes."

"It never happened before," I point out. "I was with you for several months, most of the time sleeping right here in this bed with you. This never happened, Nick."

He attempts a look of nonchalant, mild disbelief. "I'm surprised it didn't. Glad too. It's embarrassing as hell to know I stumble around in the dark and say a lot of crazy, nonsensical shit whenever I'm under stress."

"Are you under stress now?" The fact that he doesn't answer with a quick retort or a deflecting joke speaks volumes. "Am I adding stress to your life?"

"No. Never." He cups the back of my head and pins

me with a solemn stare. "You're my touchstone, Avery. My only true peace. Being with you makes everything else bearable."

"What is everything else?"

More silence, then his cell phone begins to ring again.

He rolls away from me on a curse to mute the interruption. For a long moment his head hangs down, staring at the screen. On another curse, more virulent this time, he slaps the device onto the nightstand.

I push up onto my forearm, staring at his bowed back. "Are you having issues at the office? Sounds like someone really wants to reach you this morning."

He grunts, seated on the edge of the bed. "It'll be a cold day in hell first."

The venom in his tone takes me aback. We're not finished with our conversation but he stands up, casting me a remorseful glance. "I need a shower. I'm ripe from those fucking night sweats."

A knot forms in my throat as I look up at him. I want to tell him to stay, scream at him to talk to me, to let me in.

If he pretends this isn't important, if he simply walks away—even if it's just into the next room—it will be impossible for me to believe that we'll ever get past this moment.

After what happened last night, all of the strides we've made together will be for nothing if he can't trust me with his heart . . . with the secret I dread he's been keeping since he was a boy.

"Avery," he says gently, catching my chin on the edge of his hand. "We'll talk some more. I just . . . give me a little time to sort it out, all right?"

I nod, relief leaking out of me in a heavy sigh. "All right."

His palm curves along the side of my face, his eyes filled with tender regard. "All right."

Mesmerized and so in love my chest aches with it, I watch him stroll toward the bathroom. He's just disappeared into the spacious en suite when his phone goes off again.

"I got it." I reach over and grab the device, thinking I'll just run it to him in the bathroom and he can decide what to do with the persistent caller who's apparently not about to give up anytime soon.

But then I glance down at the screen and my heart does a small freefall when I see the Florida area code. It could be anyone, but given the way Nick has been acting—given the awful way I found him last night—I know this call isn't coming from just anyone.

He's already come back out of the bathroom by the time I take a handful of steps away from the bed, the phone held numbly in my hand. I lift my head and our eyes meet. I'm sure that mine look confused, questioning.

His look is rueful. Haunted.

Resigned.

The phone is still ringing when I hand it to him.

He silences it without even glancing at the display. "My father had a stroke five years ago. I understand it was debilitating. He never recovered, and since then he's been living in a nursing home south of Miami."

Nick's voice is toneless, as if he's talking about the weather, not the man who raised him, mistreated him . . . nearly killed him the day Nick and he fought for the last time.

"They tell me his dementia has gotten worse in recent months. Apparently he doesn't remember anymore that we hate each other. Or, hell, maybe he does. For the past couple of months he's been calling me, but since the bastard can't talk anymore he just sits there on the other end of the line. Breathing. Waiting. Fucking with my head."

I walk toward him, trying to find a way to reopen our earlier conversation without pushing him too quickly. I don't want him to shut me out. "Does the nursing home know this?"

He nods tightly. "His caregivers at the home think it would do him good to have contact with family. Lucky me, I'm it."

"What did you tell them?"

"I told them I don't give a damn about what might be good for him. I told them they could tell the son of a bitch I said so."

A memory niggles at the back of my mind. Something I've hardly thought of until now. "That morning at my house, Nick . . . after you spent the night. When I came downstairs you were on the phone with someone and those were almost your exact words. That's who you were talking about? Your father?"

He clutches the phone in his fist, his expression taut with leashed anger. And pain.

I look at the torment in his handsome face and there's no need to ask how long he's been suffering night terrors again. I have no doubt they started around the same time his father began trying to reach him.

"What the fuck does he want from me, Avery? After all this time, does he think we can patch up a lifetime of despisement?" He scoffs brittly. "Does he actually expect he can mistreat me for the first eighteen years of my life then come looking for sympathy because he's rotting away in a nursing home somewhere? Or isn't he satisfied that he already fucked me up enough?"

I close the distance between us as he speaks, yearning to ease the agony that's festering inside him. I want to obliterate the demons that are destroying the man I love.

But in order to do that, first Nick is going to have to face them.

"Maybe those are questions you need to ask your father."

He glares at me as if I've betrayed him just with the suggestion. "Ask him?"

It's not easy to hold his outraged glower. Our connection is too strong. I feel his anguish and fury simply by looking at his face. And I know something of what he's going through because I've been in a similar hell.

One that Nick helped see me through at a time when I was certain I'd never fully heal. I had an ugly secret, too, and if not for him it would still be eating me alive.

"I know what it's like to carry pain and hatred in your heart," I remind him. "It's corrosive. It's self-administered poison, Nick. The only one it harms is you."

"I can't face him again, Avery. I don't care what he thinks he wants or needs from me now that he's on death's door. We've already said everything we have to say to each other. I've got the goddamn scars to prove it."

"Nick," I say softly. "I don't want you to go down there for him. Do it for yourself."

He shakes his head, his gaze shuttering even before

he's considered it. "I don't need anything from the bastard now. He had his chance to be a father. Hell, he had his chance to be a decent human being, but evidently even that was asking too much. I don't need answers from him, if that's what you think. I sure as fuck don't need his apologies."

"I know you don't." I reach out to him, resting my palms against his chest. "But I think you need to forgive him. If you and I are going to try to build a future together, you need to find a way free from the pain your father caused you."

Something dark flickers over his features now. I can't name the emotion, and when I try to study it more closely, Nick blinks and it's gone. He's put it away now, somewhere he doesn't want me to find it.

My heart aches to see that subtle withdrawal. If we stand any chance of making it this time, he needs to trust that he can show me all of who he is.

He needs to be able to take me into the darkest corners of his past and know that I won't ever leave him.

"I know what I'm asking isn't easy for you. It won't be easy for me to see you hurting either." I hold his face, imploring him to see how much he means to me. "But I also can't watch this issue between you and your father destroy the man I love. I love you so much, Nick. That's why I'm asking you to do this. For you. For me. I need you to do this for us."

"If I go . . . I don't know what I'll find there."

The sober confession is so vulnerable it brings the prickle of tears to the backs of my eyes.

"I know you don't. And I know how terrifying that must be." I rest my cheek against his sternum, listening to the strong, steady beat of his heart. "But you won't have to do it alone. I'm going with you. We're going to do this together."

24

Three days later, Avery's hand rests warmly in mine as we walk together into the sand-colored brick building in Homestead where my father has lived for the past five years.

Of course, *lived* is a relative term. As Avery and I are greeted by a distracted twenty-something receptionist then directed toward the wing of the institution that's reserved for full-time nursing care, I can't help feeling the smallest pang of pity for the old man.

After spending his whole life on the water down in the Keys, this taupe-walled maze of corridors and sickrooms must feel like a damn prison.

A monotonous, prolonged state of hell.

Not that he hasn't earned his piece of it in many ways.

Although to be fair, he isn't the only Baine man to deserve a stint in hell.

"You must be Dominic," says a heavy-set woman with big hair and a kind smile as we arrive at the attendant station in my father's area of the home. The woman shakes my hand, then Avery's, introducing herself as the afternoon floor manager. "I have to say, we were surprised to hear you were coming. And so soon. I'm sure it'll mean a lot to Bill to know you're here."

It feels bizarre to hear her mention my father with such familiarity, as if she knows him. As if she actually cares about the surly son of a bitch. Maybe the stroke mellowed him.

Then again, William Baine only seemed to have problems getting along with his own son. Just another of the reasons I learned to hate him at a young age.

The woman gestures for Avery and I to follow her. "How long has it been since you came to see him, Dominic?"

"I haven't. My father and I aren't close."

"I see." I don't miss the trace of judgment in her tone. It's also in the flick of her gaze, the slight compression of her lips.

As we walk the length of the hallway, Avery's fingers flex in my grasp, a reassuring reminder that she's with me. That she will remain with me every step of this dubious journey.

I don't realize how rapidly my heart is pounding, how damp my palms have gotten, until we're approaching a room with a closed door. Its gauzy beige curtain is drawn across the narrow pane of glass, shrouding the unlit room and its lone occupant. To the right of the doorjamb is a removable name plate that reads William "Bill" Baine.

It's been sixteen years since I saw him; now all that separates us is a few feet of pitted linoleum tile and the door I'll have to walk through on my own volition.

The attendant lowers her voice. "Before you go in, I feel I should warn you that your father's not doing well. He's been declining for some time. I, ah, I don't know if anyone has told you, but he's in the early stages of kidney failure now. Usually that means we're down to a matter of weeks before his organs begin to fail."

"Yes." I nod. "I'm aware."

I feel Avery's tender gaze on me, her soft inhalation when she hears this news for the first time. We haven't spoken of what this trip will entail or what might wait for me on the other side of this door. She's given me endless patience this week, allowing me all the time and space I need to sort out my feelings in preparation for this trip.

More importantly, she's given me her love.

"Just so you understand, Dominic, even if your father is awake, he won't be able to speak to you. But he can hear, so whatever you'd like to say to him, know that he will understand even if he no longer has the ability to express himself or respond."

I grunt, struck by the irony.

After all the times his words wounded me, now it's my turn to pay him back.

The woman looks at her watch, then offers me a polite smile. "I'll be at the nursing station where we just came from if you need anything. Take all the time you need."

Avery and I stand there for a long moment once

211

we're alone. My feet feel rooted to the floor. My lungs seem to be drying up, making it difficult to get air.

"Are you okay?" Avery's touch is feather light on my cheek. "If you're not ready to do this now, we can come back—"

"I'm ready." I brush my lips against hers in a brief kiss as I release her hand.

"I love you," she says, clutching my face in her gentle palms. "I'm going to be right out here the whole time."

My nod feels shaky. So does my hand as I reach for the latch on the door. The tangle of scars turn white as I grip the cold metal lever and push the panel open.

The room is dark. So fucking quiet.

An empty bed sits closest to the door, but I hardly notice it as I approach the other one—the one containing a shriveled shape swathed in white sheets and a thin wheat-colored blanket.

I'm not going to lie, the sight of my father lying there is a shock.

The once tall, muscular man with jet hair like my own is so far diminished I never would have recognized him. Matted gray hair covers a skull cloaked in spotted, yellowed skin. Eyes I know to be the same bright blue as mine are closed in sleep, and the mouth that used to snarl such explosive, ugly things to me now sags on the left side, lasting evidence of the stroke that sent him to this place five years ago.

I am struck by his incapacitation, by how small he seems compared to the raging monster from my youth. His unmoving body is beyond thin, the long legs that used to carry him so agilely on the deck of his fishing boat now look skeletal beneath the sheets, incapable of supporting even his diminished weight. Stretched out along his sides, his arms are mottled with the bruising of old age and blood-thinning medicines.

The powerful fists that struck me only once—that last night I was in his house—lay gnarled and bony at the ends of his wrists like useless claws.

"Jesus Christ."

An astonishing sense of sorrow swamps me as I stand beside his sleeping form. I don't want to feel sympathy for him. After all, he never had any for me. He never had anything in his heart for me except animosity.

And doubt.

This last thing was the one that cut me the deepest. It's the thing that moves me to speak to him now, even though he's snoring quietly, fully asleep.

"Are you in pain, old man?" My voice is low and hoarse with unwanted emotion as I stare down at him in the bed. "I wanted to think you would be. I thought I wanted to see you suffering."

I take a breath and I'm shocked to hear the catch in my throat. I don't want to feel anything for the uncaring bastard. I want to look at him with the same detachment, the same neglect that he always showed me.

But I can't.

"You were my father, you son of a bitch," I whisper thickly. "You were supposed to be there for me. You were supposed to protect me."

I swallow past the knot of anguish and rage that I've been carrying inside me since I was an eleven-year-old boy. Its bitter taste fills my mouth now, as acrid as poison.

"You were supposed to love me. Goddamn you, Dad. You should've kept me safe from him."

At that choked accusation, my father stirs on the

mattress. His eyes stay closed, but I can see that his mind is wading through the cobwebs of sleep. Somewhere inside that shriveled shell of a man, he knows how he failed me.

Not only as a child, when I admired him and wanted to be like him. But later too. After my mother was gone and I was a grieving kid in need of kindness. So hungry for comfort I would have turned to anyone . . . and did, only to learn it came at an unthinkable cost.

I needed my dad years later, when I was a self-destructive, messed up teen. He wasn't there for me then, either. Always pushing me away. Always ensuring I only had cause to avoid him, to hate him.

Hot tears streak down my face. I swipe at them angrily, furious with myself that once again—even after all this time—my father has reduced me to the weakling he always believed I was.

"Fuck."

This is not what I wanted to do here. I didn't come down here to cry at my father's bedside. I sure as hell didn't come here to cry for myself.

I glance over my shoulder toward the closed door. Avery leans against the wall on the opposite side of the corridor, her face turned askance, granting me the privacy she promised.

I didn't have a plan for what I would say to him, or even what I hoped to hear. I still don't know why I've come, other than to prove to her that I could.

For her—*for us*—I would do anything. I want to. But I can't do this.

Not in front of him, even if he doesn't realize I'm here.

I can't do this in front of her.

Now that I'm in here, all I want to do is get the hell out of the room.

"Shit." Shamed, I turn my face into my arm, drying my cheek on the short sleeve of my shirt. "You win, Dad. You were right. I'm a fucking pussy, just like you always said."

I turn away from the bed and stalk out of the room on a harsh curse.

"Nick?" Avery's confused, then disappointed look as I exit to the hallway just about kills me.

I don't pause to explain. I can't. "I need to get out of here."

"Okay."

She falls in at my side, hurrying along with me as my feet guide me on a swift, urgent path out of the building. I don't breathe again until I'm in the parking lot.

Then, once I'm out of the medicinal stench of the building, all of the air in my lungs explodes out of me in a violent, wracking sob.

25

Nick's hands seem frozen to the steering wheel of our rental. The engine of the Porsche is running, but we haven't yet left the nursing home parking lot. He's barely uttered a word since we got into the car.

I've been quiet, too, giving him time to process. Waiting for him to decide it's safe to open up and let me in. All I know is that his father slept through the brief visit. Nick almost seems relieved by that fact. Based on how distressed he was when he came out of the room, I can only imagine how difficult it would be for him to face the man when he was awake.

My heart still reverberates with the sound of his soul-wrenching sob. I want to hold him, but all I see when I look at him now is his urge to escape. His mind seems fixed on a point that's somewhere a million miles away from where he and I sit.

Or maybe not that far at all.

I think he's still trapped in a place located somewhere back in the Keys. One Nick thought he'd left behind him when he was eighteen years old.

I look at him and I'm terrified that he'll remain trapped in that awful place forever.

"We should go," he murmurs without looking at me.

When he puts his hand on the gearshift, I cover his fingers with mine. "Go where?"

"Home. Back to New York. I'll phone ahead to my pilot so he can file a flight plan for us."

"Nick." I keep my hold on his hand, giving him no choice but to look at me. "I don't think leaving right now is a good idea."

"I sure as hell don't want to stay here."

"I know," I offer gently. "But I think you have to. This isn't over. It won't be until you put all of your demons to rest."

He scoffs. "The only demon I have left to contend with is the shriveled bastard lying in that nursing home. Far as I'm concerned he's right where he belongs. And now I want us to go back to where we belong."

"I can't do that, Nick."

His face hardens, brows coming together in a scowl. "I need you to."

"No." I shake my head. "No, that's not what you need. You need to confront the things that happened to you in your past. All of them, Nick. I think you need to go back to the place it all began."

The curse that rips from his throat is vicious. "I'm not going back there. I can't."

"You can." I stroke the scarred hand and the knuckles that have gone white from his iron grasp on the gearshift. "You came here to try to forgive your father. If you weren't able to do that today, then maybe you need to find some way to understand him . . . and what he did."

"What he did?"

I search for gentle words, even though I know there's no soft way to bring up the subject of Nick's abuse. But does he really think I haven't been able to see the obvious signs? I've been there too. I see my broken pieces reflected in him every time I look into his eyes.

"Nick . . . I know you were harmed when you were young. You can tell me. You know I'll understand. You know it won't diminish anything I feel for you."

His head snaps back slightly, as if his mind is just returning to the here and now. "You think my father raped me?" He glances down, frowning. When he looks back up at me, there is a bleakness in his eyes that breaks my heart. "It wasn't my father, Avery. It was his father. My grandfather."

~ ~ ~

I haven't seen the old house on Key Largo since I was eighteen.

Parked in the overgrown, weed-choked dirt driveway in front of it now, it looks like a nightmarish relic from a swamp monster horror film set. Fitting, I think, as I cut the engine on the rental car and stare out at my childhood home through the windshield.

"Are you ready?" Avery asks from the passenger seat.

I don't imagine I will ever be ready to reenter the scene of my own nightmares. But I nod at her and open the door. We climb out together and she meets me in front of the vehicle, taking my hand.

I can feel her apprehension as we walk toward the sagging front porch of the waterfront bungalow. It's still daylight out, so the house is visible in all its neglected glory. In the five years since my father has been at the nursing home, it's obvious that no one has kept the place up.

The canopy of moss-draped trees are scraggly and brown. The tall swamp grasses in the yard have long gone to seed. The bungalow had been painted crisp white by my mother's own hands before she got sick. Now the wood and cinderblock structure is peeled and weathered to a dingy gray.

As we approach, I catch Avery straining to see past the modest place I was raised to the other, bigger house that looms behind it on a small incline. If it could be called a house anymore. As bad as my childhood home looks, this other one is completely uninhabitable.

The broad stairs leading to the entrance of the pillared home are caved in, inaccessible. The roof has been crushed by a huge oak, most likely uprooted during an old storm. Windows in front gape like a toothless grin. The house is monstrous and even though it's obviously vacant, I have a hard time allowing my gaze to linger on it.

"My grandparents lived there," I tell Avery before she has to ask me. "The old captain's house and the land it's built on has been in the Baine family for generations."

Only now does her gait falter. Her look is grim with

comprehension. "He lived right in your backyard?"

I shrug, but the movement feels forced. "He and my father fished together on their boat every day for more than thirty years."

She doesn't move, just stares at me for a long, painful moment. "Nick, does your father know what happened to you?"

"He knows."

As averse as I am to enter the bungalow, now that we're here I can't seem to stop my feet from taking me inside. Avery and I climb the two cement steps to the front door. My father never locked it, but even if he had the rotted frame wasn't going to prevent anyone from breaking in.

Not that there is anyone here to worry.

Silt and sawdust from the termites that have likely infested the place explode in a soft cloud as I push the door open. Inside, the house is musty and dank, abandoned.

"Watch your step," I tell Avery as we step onto the creaky, dust-covered floor of the vestibule.

A short hallway leads through the center of the house to the kitchen. Off to the left is the living room and a connected formal dining room that we never used after Mom was gone. To the right, a staircase leads to two bedrooms on the second floor and a trapdoor that opens into the attic.

I notice the pale carpet runner is the same as it was when I was a kid. Beneath years of neglect, I can still see the splotch of dark paint I spilled on the third step during the summer after fifth grade. The rusty stain looks like blood. I know that's what's on Avery's mind when I see her glance at it too.

"I was painting in the kitchen while Dad was out fishing. I lost track of time, and when I realized he would be coming in soon, I hurried to put my things away before he saw them."

She nods, already familiar with the fact that my father disapproved of my love for art. "Did he ever see any of your work? It seems like if he saw your talent—"

"He wasn't interested in anything I did, least of all my painting." I shrug, leading her away from the stairs and further into the house.

"You said your mother was a painter. Did he disapprove of her art too?"

"No. He adored her and everything about her. I suppose the only thing she did that didn't earn his approval was me." When Avery tilts her head in question, I fill in the blanks. "He told me more than once that he never wanted kids. He was thirty-six when he met my mom while delivering some sea bass to a hotel in Miami. They got together and she ended up pregnant soon afterward. If not for that, I don't think he ever planned to marry, either."

We end up in the kitchen, even though I have nothing specific to see in the house. I'm shocked to see the small breakfast table. It seemed so much larger when my dad was hunched over it drinking a glass of Jack like it was morning coffee while he paged through the newspaper.

One of those papers is folded neatly on the table, yellowed and curling up at the edges. Next to it is an empty, salt-filmed juice glass. Both items waiting for him to return, as if he has just stepped away for a few minutes not five years.

For some reason I pity the man now that I'm

stepping through the remnants of his empty, angry life. I walk over to toss the old paper. When I drop it into the open trash can at the end of the counter, I disturb the mouse and her half a dozen babies who have made their nest behind the bin.

Avery yelps as the rodents scatter around her feet. I can't hold back my chuckle as she flees the kitchen for the apparent safety of the dining room as if a herd of wild animals were chasing her.

"It's okay, they're gone," I call to her. "You can come back."

But she doesn't.

"Avery?" Now I'm the one gripped by sudden, irrational fear. I bolt for the dining room.

And find her standing inside, her gaze riveted to a framed piece hanging on the wall.

"Is this one of your mother's paintings?"

When I step beside her I feel all of the blood drain out of my head. I can't believe what I'm seeing.

"No. It's not hers. It's one of mine."

"One of yours?" She places her hand on my back, gaping as openly as I am. "If this is one of yours, Nick, then does that mean—"

"It's the only one left."

My voice is wooden, but I can't help it. I only had five paintings I was proud enough of to keep when I got out of the hospital and finally left this place for good. I took those five paintings with me to New York. A couple of years later I destroyed them all, consequences of my own pointless anger at Kathryn . . . and myself.

I thought this one had been destroyed too.

Not by me, but by my father the night we fought just a few paces from where I stand with Avery now.

I'm in complete shock to see my painting again. Even more so, to see it hanging in the old man's house.

I stare at the expressionist painting of a white bird soaring over the surface of crystalline blue water, its feathers just skimming the waves. Above the glorious wings, a brilliant sunset explodes in vibrant shades of gold. I remember working on this piece, my sense of accomplishment in seeing my vision of fire and water and the slim plane of harmony that exists between them take shape on my canvas. I had been ridiculously proud of this one.

Avery rests her head against my shoulder as she studies my work. "You painted him too. Icarus."

"Yes." I smile, turning my head to press a kiss to hers. "I can't believe it's here. That he kept it. I thought he threw it away after he ruined it that night."

She looks at me, frowning. "What night?"

"The night we fought over there in the living room."

"That's the room? That's the window that he—"

I nod, my scarred hand clenching at the memory.

"Tell me what happened, Nick."

I see the night playing out in my mind as I reach up and carefully remove my painting from the wall. I set it down on the dining room table, my breath gusting out of me on a long, heavy sigh.

"I was eighteen and I'd been out drinking with a group of friends at some rich fuck's house party down by Tavernier. I noticed he had a lot of art on the walls. Some of it was shit, but some of it was good. Really good. We started talking and I told him that I painted too. I told him as soon as I saved up some money I was going to move to Miami and try to make a go of it with my work, and he said he'd like to see what I had. He said

223

to bring my best piece around in the morning and maybe he'd buy it."

At my side, Avery glances at me cautiously. "This painting?"

"I didn't want to wait until morning. I didn't want to take the chance that he might change his mind in the meantime. So I went home. Dad was already stinking drunk when I got here. He started in on me about where I'd gone and a dozen other complaints he felt he had to air. I told him I didn't have time for his bullshit and I ran upstairs to get my work."

Avery leans against the table so that she's facing me, her expression tender but etched with dread.

"He followed me upstairs, carrying a glass of bourbon. The way he was talking and swaying on his feet I figured he'd already had several before I got home. I made the mistake of telling him what I was doing, the interest someone had in my art. I thought it might get him off my back but it only made him nastier."

"Nastier, how?" She asks when it takes me a moment to decide how to continue. How much I should say. "Nick . . . what did he say to you?"

I choke out a brittle laugh. "He went back to one of his favorite cuts—that the last thing he wanted was to raise a son who was a pussy. That I needed to forget about painting and toughen up or life was going to chew me up and spit me out. He said he didn't want to have some artsy fag for a son, that for my own good I needed to get my hands dirty like a real man. Like him and his father."

Avery winces. "Jesus."

"He was drunk," I say, unsure why I feel the need to defend him. "I'd never seen him so wasted. So fucking belligerent. But I was drunk too. I lost it. Before I knew it, I was saying things I'd never said to him before. 'You want me to be a real man, huh? A real man like you, a disgusting drunk and a pitiful excuse for a father? Or maybe you think I ought to be a real man like your father, is that it? A sick monster who gets off on fucking little boys.'"

Avery's eyes close briefly, but not before a tear leaks down her face. "Oh, Nick."

She reaches for me, and it takes all of my willpower to stand still and accept her comfort. I'm vibrating with anger at these memories. But I can't stop them from flooding in now.

"I'll never forget his expression. His entire face just . . . sagged. As if it were melting because of what I'd said. Then his fury erupted. He called me a liar. He said I was making it up, just trying to hurt him." I laugh absurdly at the idea. "Jesus Christ, as if what happened to me would hurt him at all. He exploded. Just fucking lost his mind with rage. He threw the glass of bourbon at me, but I ducked out of the way. Instead of hitting me, it smashed against my painting."

My right hand moves to the small tear that's been patched from underneath but is still present in the canvas. The faint stain of thrown whiskey still darkens some of the purity of the bird's feathers.

"He ruined it," I state flatly. "I couldn't take it to the man who might have bought it after that. My father destroyed my work. He destroyed my first potential chance to get out of this godforsaken swamp. With or without the painting, I decided I was going to leave that night. Why the fuck didn't he just let me go?"

"What did he do?"

"He followed after me when I headed back downstairs to the living room. He kept calling me a liar, telling me what I said about my grandfather wasn't true. But it was true. All of it. How could he not see the evil in his father? He spent practically every day of his life on a boat with the asshole. He had to know something of what his father was really like, didn't he?"

She slowly shakes her head, seemingly at a loss for words. There are no words that can change what happened. Nothing can be said that will erase the damage.

"I wanted to hurt the old man the way his denial was hurting me. So I told him everything. I gave him details—ugly ones. Graphic ones. I didn't spare him a thing. Not even when he started hitting me, telling me to shut the fuck up. I just kept talking. I told him how it started—Grandpa inviting me to his house after Mom died, telling me I could cry in front of him if I felt like it, that he wouldn't make fun of me the way Dad did. He started touching me soon after that. He said it was okay because we were family. Then the other stuff began. I described it all to my father, delighting in his repulsion, in the anger he couldn't control. At some point, I remember thinking that I just wished he'd finally kill me. If he wanted to shut me up, deny everything I had experienced, why didn't he just fucking end me right there? The next thing I knew, I was crashing through that window. "

"Oh, my God," Avery murmurs, her voice catching. "Nick, I'm so sorry. I'm sorry for what you went through. I'm sorry that your father refused to believe you—that he could hurt you like that."

I scoff. "The fact that he called me a liar was worse

than the rest of it. Worse than the injury to my hand and arm. Worse than the loss of my art."

She nods, and I know she understands. Avery, of all people, understands what I'm feeling and how hard it's been to keep all of this inside for so long.

Her touch is a warm comfort, her gaze fierce and loving. "You haven't lost all of your art, Nick. He kept this for you." She grows quiet, considering in silence for moment. "Nick, maybe he was sorry for what he did to you that night."

Could that be true? It's almost impossible for me to fathom. The old man never said he was sorry. Not for that night. Not for a goddamn thing.

I glance at my depiction of Icarus lying on the table. "I never thought I'd see this again. It was gone when I got home from the hospital after my injury. I just assumed he'd thrown it away."

"It looks like he tried to restore it."

I nod, feeling oddly numb as I run my finger over the crude repairs. Why would he bother? Why would he keep it on his wall when he couldn't stand the idea of me painting when I actually lived here?

I may never have those answers. I doubt I'll ever be able to comprehend my father's animosity toward me or his vehement denials of everything I told him.

But Avery was right that I needed to see this house again. I needed to walk through this place and realize there's nothing left here that can hurt me.

Not my father's confounding hatred of me.

Not even the hideous memories of what my grandfather did to me.

None of those things can touch me so long as Avery is standing at my side.

I kiss her, holding her close for a long while. "Thank you."

"For what?"

"For loving me. For being with me. I never would've come here if not for you." I press my lips to her forehead. "You were right, Avery. I had to do this. I'm glad I did. And now I'm ready to leave."

"Yes." She smiles lovingly and nods. "But not without this."

She carefully picks up the framed painting and a puzzled look comes over her face.

"What's wrong?"

"I don't know. There's something—" She turns the frame around.

Taped to the back of it is a yellowed envelope. One bearing my name and the address of Baine International's office in New York, written in my father's bold scrawl.

"What the hell?" I remove the envelope and lift the brittle seal. "There's a letter inside."

I take it out and unfold the single sheet of handwritten words.

My father's words, a confession dated only weeks before his stroke.

26

Nick's father is awake when we arrive at his room the next morning.

His bed is tilted up to a reclined sitting position, his head turned away from the door. He doesn't seem to notice that we've stepped inside. His breathing remains slow and even. His frail body unmoving.

We spent the night in an area hotel, though I don't think Nick got more than a couple hours of sleep. Twice I woke to find him pensively pacing in the dark. Before the sun came up he was already showered and dressed, seated on the hard-cushioned sofa with his father's letter unfolded in his hands.

He must have a hundred questions for the old man slouched on the bed inside this room. We are here with the full awareness that we won't get answers now. Everything William Baine might have said to his son throughout his life is contained in the five-year-old letter Nick has likely memorized by now.

As we walk into his father's room, Nick is silent, as if studying him through a new and unfamiliar lens. When the grizzled old face finally swivels in our direction, I see drawn and sallow cheeks that contain traces of the younger, handsomer face I adore. The straight line of the nose. The squared jaw. The startlingly bright blue eyes that stare warily at us as we approach.

There is a guest chair next to the bed. Nick offers it to me but I shake my head. I'll stand with him. I will always stand with him, no matter what he has to face.

Nick clears his throat. "I came yesterday, but you were asleep."

No warm greeting. Just a flat statement of facts. My heart squeezes to hear the distance that exists between the man I love and the one who fathered him.

"This is Avery," he says. "She's the reason I'm here."

Nick glances at me, the intensity of his gaze telling me that he doesn't simply mean I'm the reason he's in this room. He means something deeper than that. I squeeze his hand, hoping he understands that he means the same to me.

I look down at the fragile, dying old man in the bed and it's hard to reconcile him with the father who pushed his son away so harshly and repeatedly. At least now I know why.

I give him a slight nod of acknowledgment. "Hello."

He doesn't respond. His guarded gaze slides back to Nick as if he's bracing for a confrontation he fully expects is coming.

"I spent a lot of years being angry with you," Nick says, his deep voice toneless and unreadable. "I spent almost two decades being afraid of you. Hating you."

His father's face is stoic, but those brilliant blue eyes are filled with uncertainty. Even fear.

Nick frowns, slowly shaking his head. "Growing up, all I wanted was to be close to you. I couldn't understand why you despised me. I kept trying to figure out what I did. I knew you never wanted me. You never made a secret of that."

His father's wiry salt-and-pepper brows furrow. He emits a small moan, his head starting to move side to side against the pillow.

"No," Nick says. "Now you have to listen to me. It's my turn to talk."

I place my hand on his shoulder, trying to gentle him, anchor him. I know he's still angry and hurting. He might carry those scars forever. But he came here with things to say. Things he needs to release while he still has the chance to be heard.

He blows out a harsh breath, then tries again. "You were not a good father. I'm not even sure you were a good man. I was sure you couldn't be, not when you could say the many hateful things you said to me, your constant ridicule and denigration, the torment that seemed designed to push me away. What kind of father does that? What kind of man?"

William Baine's slack mouth quivers mutely as his son speaks. He grows agitated, frustration in his eyes.

"I asked myself those questions every day. How could my own father be so viciously determined to turn me into a heartless, uncaring bastard like himself? Why was he working so fucking hard to push me away?"

231

The sound his father makes is a strangled one, as if he's choking on all the words he's unable to form.

"Because that is what you were doing," Nick says quietly. "You were trying to make me tough. You wanted to push me away. You had to. Not because you hated me. But because you were afraid to love me. You were scared shitless that deep down, you might turn out to be the same kind of monster your father was."

There is no more struggling to speak. He freezes now, profound misery in his saggy, aged face.

"Avery and I went out to the house yesterday. We found the painting. We found your letter."

His father's eyes close. A quiet sob bubbles from between parched lips.

Only then does Nick reach out to touch the old man, resting his hand on the bony shoulder that's now wracked with tremors as his father struggles with emotions that stay clogged in his throat.

"I wish you would have told me that you'd been hurt by him too. Christ, I wish you'd told Mom. If anyone had known, you might have spared us both so much pain." Nick swears low under his breath. "Keeping the secret only made things easier for him to continue the sick cycle. It allowed him to move on, to prey on someone else. We could've put an end to it if you'd only found a way to tell me, Dad. Damn it, you should have warned me."

His father weeps while Nick talks. I may not have much sympathy for the way William Baine chose to handle his relationship with his son, but it's impossible not to feel some degree of pity for the anguish he's experiencing now, being forced to hear firsthand how his decisions and secrets impacted his only child.

"I didn't come here today to berate you," Nick tells him. "I don't have a need to upset you. That's not why I came. I just . . . I just wanted to see you one more time."

And likely the last time, given his father's hastening decline.

Nick starts to move away from the bed. He's barely taken a step when one of the thin, mottled arms reaches for him, clawed fingers grasping Nick's ruined hand. His father's eyes lock on his, tears spilling in a free fall now.

Regret and the need for absolution are etched all over the old man's face.

"I know, Dad." Nick nods solemnly. "I can't take any of it back, either. I wish we could. I'm sorry we both had to share this horrible thing in common. As for him? I'm glad he's dead. Thank you for that."

Another sob breaks free from William Baine's trembling mouth. The anguish in his haggard face is almost unbearable to watch. But Nick stands firm. He is strong enough for both of them now.

He squeezes his father's quivering hand. "I want you to know that I'm okay. I'm happy . . . because of her." He pulls me close, under the shelter of his arm. "I came back today, Dad, because I want you to know that I understand everything you did, and why. And I forgive you."

The old man's lips part, but the only sound that escapes them is a long, rasping exhalation. I know what he's trying to say. I'm certain that Nick knows too.

I love you.

I'm sorry.

Nick extricates himself from the feeble grasp on his hand. With a tender palm, he cups the back of his father's gray head. "Be at peace now, Dad."

With a murmured goodbye, Nick turns away from the bed and gathers me close as we walk out of the room together.

27

W e've been in the air for about an hour, heading back to New York. I am seated in a leather club chair across from Avery on board the Baine International corporate jet.

My painting leans against the opposite wall from me. I still can't believe it exists after all this time. Nor have I yet come to grips with the reason why.

I have a glass of single malt in one hand, my father's letter in the other.

I've read it a dozen times at least.

I don't know how many times I'll have to read his words before they no longer open a cold hollow behind my sternum, one that leaves me feeling oddly bereft.

My father's not dead yet, but reading his letter—one penned to me under the assumption he would be gone before it reached me—makes me realize just how little I truly knew about him.

Both his cowardice, and, in the end, his courage.

I down the last swallow of whisky as my gaze travels over his jagged handwriting once more.

> *Dominic,*
>
> *If you're reading this, it means that I am dead and this letter, along with your painting, has found its way to you in New York. I realize I'm taking the easy way out here. Waiting to write this until you can't ask questions or tell me what a pussy I am for keeping all of this from you isn't fair and I'm sorry for that. I'm sorry for everything. I guess that's the main thing I need you to know.*
>
> *I wasn't fit to be a father—I doubt I need to tell you that. The thought of having kids scared the piss out me. And then I met your mother and it wasn't long afterward when she told me she was pregnant. I begged her to abort, but she wouldn't think of it. Maybe I should've told her why I didn't want to have a child. Hell, maybe I should've just packed her up and sent her back to her parents. You both would've been better off if I had.*
>
> *I'll never forget the first time I saw you in her arms. This pink, squalling thing, as helpless as a kitten. I panicked when she handed you to me. How was I going to protect something so fragile and innocent? I couldn't even protect myself from my own father. I decided then and there that I could only make sure that my son was tough enough to protect himself. I promised myself I'd raise you to be strong so no one would ever be able to break you, especially not the way I'd been broken.*
>
> *I don't recall the first time my father touched me. I only know it didn't stop until I hit puberty and got big enough to defend myself. About that same time, I worked up the guts to tell my mother what he'd done. Instead of defending me, she put a shotgun under her chin and pulled the trigger, leaving me all alone with him.*
>
> *He and I worked the boat every day from the time I could hold a fishing rod. That didn't change after you came along. I saw him looking at you one day. You were maybe seven or eight. I wanted to kill him right then and there. Now I realize*

I should have. Instead I pushed you away from the family business. To make sure you stayed away, I told you that you were weak. That you were useless.

You weren't either of those things, son. I was.

Until that night we fought here at the house, I thought you'd been spared. I can't describe how it felt to hear you say what he'd done to you. I didn't want to believe it was possible that I failed you. I was too drunk to reel in my horror—or my anger. At him. Myself. Even you, for being so trusting that he was able to get to you too.

I didn't mean to destroy your art. I never meant to strike you. When I realized what I'd done to you that night, I wanted to die. I knew I couldn't fix any of that. But I could take care of what I should've done years ago.

After you got out of the hospital and moved away, I took him out on the swamp boat. When we got far enough out, I cut the engine and told him I knew what he'd done to you. He didn't even try to deny it. I had a hunting knife and a cinder block anchor with me on the boat. I dumped his body deep enough in the swamp so the only thing that would find him were the gators. I didn't worry that anyone would miss him.

I doubt anyone's going to miss me now that I'm gone, either. Least of all you.

I'm not going to ask for your understanding. I don't dare hope you'll ever be able to forgive me. I just want you to know that I really did care, son. I really do love you.

I only wish I'd been man enough to let you know.

Your father

It takes me a moment to absorb those last few lines. I can't deny the impact they have on me, even now.

When I finally glance up from his letter, I find Avery tenderly watching me. She crosses the cabin to climb into my lap. Wrapping herself around me and holding fast, she is the embodiment of support and affection. I close my arms around her, pressing a kiss to the top of her head.

She buries her face in my chest, her voice soft and warm. "Are you all right?"

"Yeah." My fingers trace small circles on her back as she cuddles against me. "Each time I read it, I feel less anger toward him. Less of the hurt. I suppose it's hard to hate someone who's so much like yourself."

She lifts up, frowning. "You're not like him, Nick. You're not a coward—not ever. You're the bravest man I know. I witnessed that myself this morning when you stood at his bedside. Even at your worst moments, you're never cruel. Your father wanted to make you cold and tough, unreachable. You're not any of that, either."

"I was," I remind her, thinking back to the years after I first left Florida. I was angry and bitter, concerned only about my own survival. Motivated by my own narcissistic needs. "I was all of those things and worse. Until I found you."

She's smiling as I bend my head to kiss her. Laughing as I scoop her into my arms and deposit her gently beneath me on the large sofa.

"You've changed everything, Avery. You've changed me."

"Not too much, I hope. I happen to like the man you are."

I arch a brow. "You like him?"

"I love him," she says. "With everything I am, I love him."

A surge of pure, unabashed happiness rises up within me as I gaze at the extraordinary woman in my arms. In the time I've known her, I've given her a hundred reasons to walk away, and yet here she is. Trusting me. Forgiving me. Believing in me.

Loving me.

It's more than I ever dreamed I'd have in my life. Far more than I'll ever deserve. But I plan to spend the rest of my life striving to be the man I see reflected in her eyes.

"I love you too," I murmur against her lips. "With everything I am now and will ever be, Avery, I love you."

28

One month later

Nick holds the bronze urn over the side of the *Icarus* and carefully pours his father's ashes onto the crystalline water.

There are no words of soft regard offered for William Baine, no tears shed as the ocean embraces the dark gray cloud of his cremains and draws it under. This ceremony is solemn and private. Just Nick and me and the warmth of a brilliant sunrise that paints the sky in pastel shades of pink and peach and lavender.

It is a far different affair than the other funeral we attended a few weeks ago.

Unlike Nick's father, Kathryn Tremont exited her world on her own terms—the same way she lived it. Only days after we returned to New York, Kathryn's nurse had called to let us know that she had ended her own life while she was at her house in the Hamptons.

Her memorial had been an event, of course. Kathryn wouldn't have had it any other way. I wasn't surprised to learn that in absence of any heirs, her fortune and her estate had gone to the handful of her favorite charities and art museums.

But there was a special provision that had come as a shock to Nick and me.

An incredibly generous gift that we will be used to seed a brand-new non-profit venture for the construction of youth recreation centers all over the country. Andrew Beckham has already drawn up the paperwork.

But before Nick's vision goes national, he and I will be overseeing the design of a more personal project—a small oceanfront resort and sailing school for abused kids. We'll be breaking ground next year on a particular plot of land on Key Largo.

When we boarded the *Icarus* this morning, Nick told me that as far as he was concerned, that's his only pressing obligation on the mainland. Everything else can either be handled by his teams or wait for our return.

I can't help the contentment—and desire—that overcomes me as I watch him move across the deck of the beautiful sailboat. It's always like this for me when I look at him. I'm sure it always will be.

"What will we do for almost a year at sea together?" I ask him once he's put the urn away and comes back to me at the wheel.

He draws me into the circle of his arms. "I'm sure we'll think of something."

"Does that mean you have ideas?"

"Baby, I've got hundreds of them." His mouth quirks before he kisses me.

It's so easy to lose myself in the bliss of his lips on mine, his arms wrapped protectively, possessively, around me. I want to kiss him uninterrupted for days, and I can hardly contain my excitement over the fact that I can start enjoying that privilege now.

Waves roll beneath us and I groan in protest when Nick's mouth leaves mine.

"Hands on the wheel," he commands me in a low purr. "We should set our course."

I oblige him, pivoting around to take the helm with him standing at my back. "Where to, Captain Baine?"

He points over my shoulder toward the empty horizon. "We have several choices. Bermuda up there. The Bahamas and the rest of the Caribbean down that way. Or we could just go wherever the wind and the waves carry us. It's up to you."

"Anywhere at all?" I ask him, mulling over the possibilities. "And you trust me at the wheel of your baby?"

His lips press against the sensitive curve of my neck and shoulder. "I trust you with more than that, angel. I trust you with my heart."

I smile, leaning into the warmth of his body at my back. "So does that mean I'm officially your first mate now?"

"Actually, I was hoping you'd officially be my wife."

I freeze. Disbelief—and overwhelming elation—rocket through me as I let go of the wheel and turn around to face him. "What?"

"I love you, Avery. I don't ever want to know a day without you at my side."

He reaches into his pocket and retrieves a platinum engagement ring bearing a large diamond that glitters like a piece of heaven.

A stunned laugh bubbles out of me. "You came prepared?"

His smile seems shy, almost apologetic. "I was going to wait until we were somewhere romantic and tropical. I wanted it to be perfect for you, so I've been trying to think of the right words to say when I gave this ring to you."

I shake my head as I watch him slip the gorgeous ring onto my finger. My heart is soaring, my love for him spilling over in a rush of happy tears. "You already said the perfect thing. You said you love me."

"Yes, I do. I'm going to love you forever, Avery."

"Good," I tell him, twining my arms around his neck. "Because forever is only the start of how long I'm going to love you."

~ * ~

Did you miss the first book in this acclaimed
erotic romance series?

For 100 Days

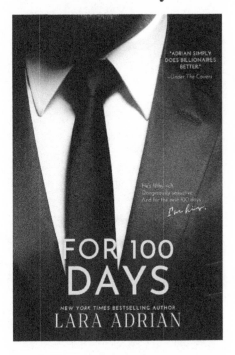

Available Now

"If you're looking for a hot new contemporary
romance along the lines of Sylvia Day's Crossfire
series then **you're not going to want to miss
this series.**"

--Feeling Fictional

You met Baine International security chief and
combat veteran Gabriel Noble in the 100 Series.
Discover his hidden scars and forbidden cravings
in this all-new novel!

Run to You

His mission is to
protect her ...
not fall in love.

RUN
to you

NEW YORK TIMES BESTSELLING AUTHOR
LARA ADRIAN
A 100 SERIES NOVEL

Available Now

Look for this 100 Series standalone novel in
ebook, trade paperback and unabridged
audiobook

You met brilliant artist Jared Rush in the 100 Series. Unravel his darkest secrets and desires in this all-new novel!

Play My Game

Available Now

Look for this 100 Series standalone novel in ebook, trade paperback and unabridged audiobook

Nick and Avery's story is also available in a 3-book digital boxset. Look for it at your favorite eBook retailer.

The 100 Series Trilogy
Digital Box Set

"For those of you looking for your next Fifty fix, look no further. I know - you have heard the phrase before - except this time it's the truth and I will bet the penthouse on it."
--*Mile High Book Club*

Never miss a new book from Lara Adrian!

Sign up for Lara's VIP Reader List at
www.LaraAdrian.com

Be the first to get notified of Lara's new releases,
plus be eligible for special subscribers-only exclusive
content and giveaways that you won't find
anywhere else.

Sign up today!

ABOUT THE AUTHOR

LARA ADRIAN is a *New York Times* and #1 international best-selling author, with nearly 4 million books in print and digital worldwide and translations licensed to more than 20 countries. Her books regularly appear in the top spots of all the major bestseller lists including the *New York Times*, USA Today, Publishers Weekly, Amazon.com, Barnes & Noble, etc. Reviewers have called Lara's books "addictively readable" (Chicago Tribune), "extraordinary" (Fresh Fiction), and "one of the consistently best" (Romance Novel News).

With an ancestry stretching back to the Mayflower and the court of King Henry VIII, the author lives with her husband in New England.

Visit the author's website and sign up for new release announcements at **www.LaraAdrian.com**.

Find Lara on Facebook at
www.facebook.com/LaraAdrianBooks

Love paranormal romance?

Read Lara's bestselling Midnight Breed vampire romance series

A Touch of Midnight
Kiss of Midnight
Kiss of Crimson
Midnight Awakening
Midnight Rising
Veil of Midnight
Ashes of Midnight
Shades of Midnight
Taken by Midnight
Deeper Than Midnight
A Taste of Midnight
Darker After Midnight
The Midnight Breed Series Companion
Edge of Dawn
Marked by Midnight
Crave the Night
Tempted by Midnight
Bound to Darkness
Stroke of Midnight
Defy the Dawn
Midnight Untamed
Midnight Unbound
Claimed in Shadows
Midnight Unleashed
Break The Day
Fall of Night
King of Midnight

Discover the Midnight Breed
with a FREE eBook

Get the series prequel novella
A Touch of Midnight
for FREE at LaraAdrian.com!

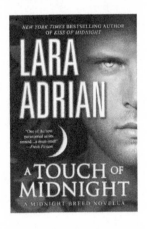

After you enjoy your free read, look for Book 1

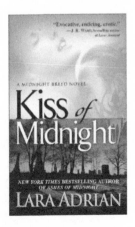

Connect with Lara online at:

Made in United States
Orlando, FL
01 June 2024

47424050R00168